... acclaimed novels, *Alma Coga...* AUG 2014 ...ne Whitbread First Novel Prize), *Fullalove* and *The North of England Home Service*. He is lso the author of the non-fiction titles *Somebody's Iusband, Somebody's Son, Pocket Money, Happy Like Murderers, On the Way to Work* (with Damien Hirst) and *Best and Edwards*.

by the same author

GORDON BURN

Born Yesterday

the news as a novel

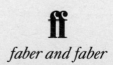

faber and faber

First published in 2008
by Faber and Faber Limited
3 Queen Square London WCIN 3AU

Typeset by Faber and Faber Limited
Printed in the UK by CPI Bookmarque, Croydon, CRO 4TD

A CIP record for this book
is available from the British Library

ISBN 978–0–571–24026–5

10 9 8 7 6 5 4 3 2 1

Carol Gorner

Man is separated from the past (even from the past only a few seconds old) by two forces that go instantly to work and cooperate: the force of forgetting (which erases) and the force of memory (which transforms) . . .

Beyond the slender margin of the incontestable (there is no doubt that Napoleon lost the battle of Waterloo), stretches an infinite realm: the realm of the approximate, the invented, the deformed, the simplistic, the exaggerated, the misinformed, an infinite realm of non-truths that copulate, multiply like rats, and become immortal.

Milan Kundera, *The Curtain*

Chapter One

The professional dog-walkers make up a loose, slightly uneasy, and yet clearly defined community within the broader community of the park. Some of them go there three and even four times a day, with up to seven or eight dogs in tow (although this contravenes a bye-law and can result in them being pulled over and given a casual warning by the parks' police who cruise the three wide carriage-drives that run parallel to the river, as well as the popular cottaging areas adjacent to the public toilets and the athletics track).

Most 'civilian' dog-walkers keep to the permanent paths which are mapped on a series of prominent, theatrical-looking, lectern-style boards which came in as part of a Lottery-funded facelift the park was given a few years ago; there are similar boards illustrating the breeds of bird in the aviary, and the varieties of trees and shrubs in the Sub-Tropical and 'English' gardens.

But because they have packs of dogs to clean up after, and most dogs prefer to do their business on a soft rather than a hard surface, the professionals tend to gravitate towards the football fields and the other open grassy areas where, in their muddy boots and slightly eccentric head-gear and greasy, saliva-slicked all-weather wear, they are as familiar a sight as the seagulls that bicker around the stud-pitted centre-circles – dark fungal pools in these days of torrential rain and summer floods – and the crows that lurk on the bare woodwork of the goals.

The dog-walkers stand around chatting in small groups which are permanently distracted by dogs that want balls thrown for them, or a food reward, or just a show of affection. They are as habitual in their behaviour as the people with them, and the sound of their barking carries across the park.

It is difficult to say exactly why, but the dog-walkers always convey a sense of being reluctantly – even resent-fully – pushed into each other's company. Perhaps it is because the park is a place of work for them instead of the recreational space it is for everybody else; another day at the office. Or maybe it is because they are too similar – middle-aged, white, well-informed, well-spoken – and see their own failings and private sadnesses reflected in each other. What pass in their lives has brought them here, to a pleasant but not particularly salubrious park in south London (a park extremely popular, it has to be said, with location units for films and television), with tersely tied supermarket bags of dogs' 'poo', as they call it, in their pockets and business cards with 'Doggy Daycare' printed on them or a van with 'Happy Tails' painted along the side?

James is the only one of the dog-walkers I know by name, and the only one whose story I know anything about. James is small and compact, with an unruly head of curly blond hair and a countryman's face, and probably grew up with the expectation of being something in the City. But something has gone wrong.

How wrong became clear when he was chosen as a subject for the television programme *How Clean Is Your House?*, whose presenting team of Kim and Aggie had become unlikely celebrities, appearing as guests on chat-shows and putting out a bestselling book of household cleaning hints. Aggie is snooty and small and disapproving; she is the straight-feed for Kim (the star of the show), who is camp and blonde and cartoon-like with her big hair and big bosoms and her marabou feather-trimmed rubber gloves, like a Dick Emery-era pantomime dame.

Both of them went into what appeared to be an unfeigned overdrive of shock and revulsion at the start of the show, which followed them as they tried to bring some sense of order to James's hole of a flat above a newsagent's in Brixton. The squalor was genuinely disturbing, almost heroic in a way. It must have been an eye-opener to his well-to-do Chelsea regulars on the other side of the river: blackened bath, dirt-encrusted kitchen sink, the furniture in the living room buried under stiffened grey drifts of used tissues, like the piles of wipe-rags that form the back-drop of certain Lucian Freud paintings. It made you wonder why he continues to carry a video copy of the programme around the park with him which he is happy to dig out of the backpack filled with his dog-walking paraphernalia and lend to anybody who expresses an interest in seeing it. And yet he seems better for the experience; purged, in a way, with a new spring in his step, a new swagger. And, as he likes to point out, he got a virtually new flat out of it.

Slightly older than James, more melancholic and more of a loner, is a man whose dogs all have a red plastic disc saying 'Houndbound', the name of his dog-sitting service, attached to their collars. Aitch, as I have come to think of him, once told me it had taken him two days to think the name up. 'I used to be stuck at home at night waiting for people to pick their dogs up', he said, 'then the landlord found out about it – after twelve years – and I had to start working out of the back of the car. Whacked the prices straight up fifty per cent.'

I once saw Mrs Thatcher, who comes to the park occasionally, stop by one of Aitch's mid-morning dawdlers – Harry, an exceptionally sweet-natured but easily distracted black brindle-coated cocker spaniel – and discreetly let the plastic 'Houndbound' tag run through her second and third fingers without comment. This is one of the techniques she has developed to protect her identity: whenever she feels she may have been spotted by a member of the public – maybe she has a sixth sense for detecting the little jump at the heart that many people experience when they run up against somebody as absurdly famous as she clearly understands herself to be, a jump that can trigger unpredictable and out-of-character responses – she looks around for a dog to pet, bending almost double so that only the crown of her head or the sheen of her scarf remain visible; failing that, she brings to her companions' attention a leaf or a flower in bud or a squirrel clinging to the trunk of a tree that she has suddenly found irresistibly interesting.

Mrs Thatcher's appearances in the park started quite soon after the official announcement of her withdrawal from public life on the advice of her doctors. Security considerations, I suppose, determine the timing and frequency of her visits and also which of the two main car parks, the one on the north side of the park or the one on the south, both of them narrow and gravelled and half a mile long, her detectives decide to use.

But on those first early sightings she was always in the part of the park closest to the river and directly opposite the area of Chelsea where she had lived for many years until she became prime minister, and where she brought up her children. On the first occasion I saw her, I remember she was standing by the rail overlooking the river and pointing with her finger in the direction of the Royal Hospital and Flood Street and the black-and-white, half-timbered, suburban-looking house which seemed to belong to a different world to the primary-coloured, energetically dissolute world of Chelsea and the King's Road going on barely fifty yards away.

The companion gazing politely across in the direction in which she was pointing that morning was somebody I took to be a nurse or a professional carer; she was wearing ordinary street clothes but she had the deferential attitude tinged with boredom of the paid listener.

Denis Thatcher, Mrs – by then, of course, *Baroness* – Thatcher's husband, had recently died (he died in 2003). The twins, Mark and Carol, were living abroad, in exile from the force-field of their mother's fearsome Boadicea qualities of power, purpose, and defiant determination. (When she won *I'm a Celebrity . . . Get Me Out of Here!* in 2005 and was asked to guess what her mother's reaction would be, Carol Thatcher replied that her mother probably didn't even know she was there. Then she added: 'I don't even have her phone number.')

So she was alone, and committed to the care of agency nurses and her close-protection officers from the Special Branch. Eventually, in the course of talking to the women who run the tea kiosk in the park, I worked out that the route the Thatcher party settled on sometimes depended less on operational considerations than more mundane ones: in the summer months a mobile van operates on the edge of the car park running alongside the river, and Mrs T's detectives occasionally can't resist the lure of a bacon sandwich. '"I know is not real bacon," he tell me, "but I can't resist smell."' Irina is a recent arrival from Lithuania; she can't do the upper-class (to her ears) English accent she would like, so she puts on a toffee-nosed expression instead. 'Well, yes', she says, 'what he especk? At this price is not organic!'

Irina and her tea-kiosk colleague, Klavdia, a Ukrainian, have had an interesting introduction to British life. The man they work for supplies vans to pop festivals and various tourist attractions and, in between their usual duties in the park, in the high season of 2007 they are attending some of the landmark events of a water-logged English summer. Two days before, it had been the Concert for Diana organised by the young princes in memory of their mother at Wembley. A week earlier, Klavdia and Irina had been part of the mud-bath at Glastonbury, where they say they worked for seventy-two hours virtually without a break. 'All the drug faces,' Klavdia remembered. 'Drug faces in long line and the rolls of the bread. Is all I see. I sleep in tent except I no sleep. Mud and noise. All different musics coming from around. Is horrible.'

'For two days I lie in bed,' Irina said. 'For two days I sleep. Then I shout my husband: Vladimir! Bring me food! I need drink! Cigarettes . . . My legs, my back. Oh! As I stand here still they hurt.'

On the one occasion when I was the next customer after the officers of Mrs Thatcher's protection squad at their counter, I asked the women when I was sure the detectives were out of earshot whether they had recognised the lady accompanying the men as our former great leader. They rose on their toes and craned their necks to take a look at the slightly crook-shouldered woman who by then was lavishing her attention on an orange Pomeranian dog that I knew went by the name 'Galliano'. They just shrugged. They were more exercised by the implied slur on the quality of the bacon – 'At this price is not organic!' – that they were putting in their sandwiches.

Her casual acquaintance with Aitch, the dog-walker, and his dogs; her association, at one remove, with the grunge and mud and drug culture of Glastonbury; her bacon-sandwich-savouring minders. All of this gave Mrs Thatcher a more human dimension. This was also the effect of course of the clothes she chose – or were chosen for her – to wear for her trips to the park. They were anonymous to the point of invisibility: a full-length camel-hair coat, a headscarf in windy weather, flat suede lace-up shoes of the kind you see advertised in the backs of the colour supplements and that at a first glance I mistook for trainers.

Gone was the heightened reality of the 'Iron Lady', scourge of the trade unions, victor of the Falklands War, the best man in the Cabinet. These were old ladies' clothes. And her hair now – on these walks at least – was nearly an old lady's hair: not grey (it still had a kind of honeyed glow), but worn close to the head with little of the volume blown and lacquered into it for her appearances in public. (It reminded me of my own mother's hair in her final years, in fact, when she would wear a transparent nylon 'snood' to bed in an attempt – increasingly futile as the week wore on – to preserve a little of the fullness of the shampoo-and-set which, sticking to a lifetime's habit, she had been given at the start of the weekend.)

On the morning I first saw Mrs Thatcher standing by the railing near the Peace Pagoda, pointing in the general direction of the place where she had lived with her husband and children (a loose gold bracelet set with cloudy garnet and other coloured stones, familiar from press photographs and her appearances on television over many years, caught the light and mingled with the strong light on the water; it was the only thing connecting this older, failing woman with the vigorous younger one) – that first sighting of the powerful world leader now looking vulnerable and frail brought back something Mrs Thatcher's former foreign-affairs private secretary Charles Powell had said after her eviction from Downing Street, in November 1990, seventeen years ago now.

With Denis, and in visible distress, tears smudging her make-up, she had been driven straight from Number 10 to the house in the unpromising-looking gated development in Dulwich which was meant to be their new home. It was from there that Mrs Thatcher called Powell after she had been out of office for a few days: she had a plumbing problem and didn't know what to do. 'Try the Yellow Pages,' is what Powell is said to have told her.

Tony Blair's boast was that he never touched a computer during his years as prime minister. He didn't own a mobile phone. He didn't need one; he was surrounded by aides with phones and pagers – battalions of people with personalised ringtones dashing about, staring into BlackBerrys and do-everything mobile devices. 'Who r u?', the reply he received to the first text he sent on the mobile he was equipped with when he stepped down as prime minister, he said was typical of his uselessness with any kind of new technology.

That was less than a week ago. Today – 3 July 2007 –

Blair has been out of office for just six days. On 24 June, at a set-piece rally in Manchester, he had finally passed the Labour leadership on to Gordon Brown. On 27 June, Brown had at last settled his craving to become prime minister. Blair had arrived at Buckingham Palace in the official armour-plated car shortly after one to tender his resignation to the Queen; he left the palace in a plain Vauxhall. A few hours later the car that picked him up at Darlington station, for the last leg of the journey to his constituency, was a rusted-out Vauxhall Omega with 42,000 miles on the clock – details that few papers failed to mention.

(A new car – bullet-proof, top-of-the-range – was currently on order from BMW in Munich. The order had been placed by the Metropolitan Police's counter-terrorism command. To ensure that its security remained uncompromised, in late September it would be delivered by transporter straight from the docks to a police garage in Vauxhall in south London, where, when the locks were thrown, it would be found to contain four illegal migrants who, like their predecessors in the nineteenth century, stepping off the boat in Liverpool believing it to be Manhattan, must have briefly, dismayingly mistaken this way-station with its prefabricated walls and oily rags for their arrival in the New World. The irony of this for Tony Blair, the man who had invested such energy in the issue of national security, the introduction of identity cards, of biometric screening and so on, was also made much of by commentators.)

But the car sent to pick him up at Darlington station was late. The early news had shown him lugging his own bag out of the first-class lounge at King's Cross and on to the train. The bag was open, bulging, a brown woollen sleeve trailing, the buckle of a strap bouncing along in the dirt.

The scene at Darlington, played out under the vaulted glass roof with its cast-iron pillars and braces, on the greasy cobbled ramp that led up to the turning-circle and the taxi rank, was a melancholy one. For Blair, the master communicator, it was a symbolic sackcloth-and-ashes moment, larded with bathos, choreographed for the cameras: that is what you wanted and now you've got it. But Cherie's face was fierce. She did the thing of twisting her watch-strap on her wrist, scowling at it and twisting it bad-temperedly again. (She had never looked like a willing visitor to the north-east and his constituency in his twenty-four years as an MP and this would be one of the last visits ever; she was out of there.) She shifted from foot to foot. A pool of liquid congealed under the bench just to the right of where she was standing. Discarded takeaway bags from Costa Coffee were looped over the spikes of the Victorian railings blunted by generation upon generation of black paint.

The cruelty of politics, as somebody once remarked, is its attraction.

I found I started looking out for Mrs Thatcher on my walks across the park, this carrier of large, significant, exciting events. I was drawn to the places I had spotted her in the past, perhaps with the thought I might write about it one day.

Today is like autumn in the park: it's warm, but the gutters are flooded; the playing fields are waterlogged and carrying standing water; the paths are littered with the splintered branches of trees brought down by a gusting overnight wind; the leaves clogging the puddles are waxy and green.

But it isn't autumn; it's early summer. Wimbledon is still in progress. It is the second Tuesday of Wimbledon, which has been a wash-out, with some matches limping on over five days. Parts of Yorkshire and the Midlands are under water. Hundreds of families are living in caravans and in emergency accommodations in squash-courts and village halls. The TV news has been running footage of flood victims in Hull tagging their washing machines and trunk freezers with aerosol paint to prevent them being looted before they can claim the insurance, like moorland animals; like electric sheep.

Do Androids Dream of Electric Sheep?, the title of a Philip K. Dick 1968 science-fiction novel, is something I have been reminded of by both this coverage of the floods and reports from Praia da Luz on the Madeleine McCann kidnapping, which have been taking turns in leading the news, and informing each other in unexpected ways.

Dick's novel was loosely adapted by Ridley Scott for his film *Blade Runner*, and the distinction between the human and the android, the organic and the artificially simulated, lies at the heart of both film and book.

The androids of the novel are made entirely of organic components and are physically indistinguishable from humans. But humans have authentic memories, and androids don't. It is by the presence of memories, and their attendant emotions, that humans are distinguished from replicants, or simulated humans. Rachel Rosen is saved at the end of *Blade Runner* by the bounty hunter Deckard acquiescing to her passionate conviction that the family photographs she possesses are indeed the source of authentic memories; she crosses over and is accepted as human.

The conviction, given wide expression in the press and across the blogosphere, that Kate McCann was 'hardly human' in the cool and controlled way she behaved in the televised appeals for information about Madeleine and in the attention she gave to her clothes and hair and other aspects of her appearance in the face of catastrophe, clearly implied that she must be implicated in some way in the disappearance of her daughter. The chief characteristic of androids is their lack of empathy. Because androids cannot feel empathy, their responses are either missing or, when faked, measurably slower than those of 'genuine' human beings.

I didn't expect to see Mrs Thatcher in the park today. For one thing, there is the weather: thunder, hail, rain, floods, occasional humid sunny periods. 'July monsoon –

Amazing pictures' will be the page-one flash in tomorrow's *Evening Standard*. In late afternoon this part of London – and so the All-England Championships at Wimbledon, where the organisers are reportedly planning a third week – will be plunged into purple apocalyptic gloom and battered with a blizzard of ice-balls as big as marbles. Hail will blanket the rooftops and streets and blow into banks and drifts against garden walls and in the lee of every tree trunk.

Far more relevant than the weather, though, in determining whether the former prime minister takes her turn in the park is the fact that the terrorist threat level has been raised to 'critical', the highest degree possible, following attempted car-bomb attacks on the West End and Glasgow airport, a tactic for inflicting mass murder – propane gas and common nails, flooring nails and roofing nails – imported, as the intelligence services had for some time been dreading, from the streets of Baghdad.

It is exactly the sort of national crisis Mrs Thatcher, who came close to being killed by the IRA at Brighton in 1984, was famous for grabbing by the throat – 'I must govern!' – and everybody is waiting now to see how Gordon Brown shapes up. ('Today we were unlucky, but remember we only have to be lucky once,' the IRA said in a statement at the time of the Brighton bombing. 'You will have to be lucky always.')

In office, Mrs Thatcher never read newspapers. She only read what her press secretary Bernard Ingham told her was in them. Out of office, though, the rumour mill insists she has all the papers brought to her every morning, when she sets about them with a marker pen, highlighting idiocies, striking through inaccuracies, furiously scribbling comments and corrections in the margins. (What happens to the marked-up articles then? Does somebody clip them and have them couriered to the relevant minister or senior civil servant? Are they indexed and annotated and transferred to a Thatcher research resource or archive, to await posthumous decoding? Or does she have her own A. J. Weberman figure, famous for picking through Bob Dylan's garbage in the hope of unearthing secret information, coiner of the term 'garbology', sniffing round the dustbins of Belgravia?)

As it is, I recognise the cars as soon as I see them sweep in off the roundabout and through the gates – a bottle-green Jaguar slung low through the weight of its own bulletproof glass and protective steel-plating, tailed by a silver Land Rover whose occupants (I know this from Irina at the tea kiosk) stay behind to keep an eye on things when Mrs T's morning constitutional is in progress.

It is the first time I have been around for this arrival part of the operation. But it is instantly familiar – Jaguar moving like a bullet through water, support vehicle bringing up the rear – from the overhead shots that tracked first Blair, and then Brown, as they made their separate ways to and from the Palace last Wednesday. (In a few weeks' time I will recognise it again, at closer quarters, when the taxi that's taking me to an appointment at the House of Commons is halted by police out-riders at the MI5 building opposite Lambeth Bridge to give the prime minister's Jag a clear run along Millbank.) Very quickly the cars are a few hundred yards away at the western end of the car park, where they stay in formation, parked parallel to the kerb, rather than poked into the bays like the smattering of other cars that are already there.

Towards the end of the long countdown to his retirement as prime minister, Tony Blair's personal detectives, some of them with him from the beginning, were given two choices: stay with him in his new role as ordinary citizen, or opt to be deployed elsewhere in the protection service. Anticipating a future based on that of his friend Bill Clinton, who he was already occasionally meeting for dinner at Claridge's, or drinks in his suite at the Ritz, or at the Mondrian in Los Angeles or the Marriott in Palm Springs or the Sherry Netherland in New York for one of Clinton's starry 'social entrepreneurship' events, based on the idea that business and philosophy can form a seamless whole (motto: 'Using entrepreneurial methods and market mechanisms to solve social problems') – looking forward to an easy life on the international charity and lecture circuits, Tony's detectives (motto: 'I'll have what he's having') had all signed up to stay with Tony. Only to have it announced on the day of his last appearance in Parliament that, far from chasing the high life, Blair had angled for and been given the job of special peace envoy to the Middle East. So it was goodbye candle-lit cosy-ups with Brangelina and Bono (the heavies know probably better than anybody that among the most visible benefits of celebrity is access to fellow celebrities; also that their own darkling presence is one of the most potent modern signifiers of status). It was goodbye to that, and hello street skirmishes and local militias and a future of dodging bombs and ducking bullets at checkpoints and sandbagged shit-holes in the occupied territories. There was a rush to jump ship as soon as Blair's peace envoy role was announced. But his detectives were told they had signed up and were committed; they were there for the duration and to please collect their body armour on the way out.

Mrs Thatcher of course knows this. Even in this period of her senescence, she gives the impression of still knowing everything. A fortnight ago she had taken Tony Blair's arm at a memorial service to mark the twenty-fifth anniversary of the Falklands war, one of his last showpiece appearances as prime minister. (She had caused a kerfuffle by turning up in a lavender hat-dress-and-coat outfit virtually identical to the one worn by her old adversary, the Queen.) In a few days, waiting for the start of the Wimbledon semifinal between X and Y, I will glance up from the paper to see her easing past Terry Wogan in the royal box at Wimbledon, inclining her head to take the applause, raising her hand in a small regal wave once she is seated.

Where does she go in between all the times she is not being 'Margaret Thatcher'? The answer, sometimes it seems, is here, where the short, purposeful steps of her performance self are allowed to dwindle into the short, tentative steps of pensionerdom and widowhood and she is allowed time away from the big, emphatic colours she uses to identify herself for the cameras – her blazons.

I watch them form up into the usual group – the two women in the middle, dressed virtually identically, a protection officer front and rear, narrow diamond formation – and move slowly from the car park, across the carriage-drive with its steep camber and submerged gutters, in the direction of the lake.

The detectives assigned to her have grown old in her service. With their mottled cheeks and serge overcoats and tightly rolled umbrellas, they could be middle-ranking civil servants or (the slightly younger, slightly more dashing ones, the type she has always had an eye for – the type Mark Thatcher has always tried to emulate, shirts from Turnbull & Asser, shoes from Lobb, hoping for his mother's approval) denizens of the secret world of intelligence.

A shelter squats between the Thatcher party and the lake, largely blocking the path, making the path fork around it. Open to the weather on four sides, with a metal hasp-anchored timber bench in each, it has been graffitied over and had names gouged out of it of course, and attracts what are known among the more respectable users of the park as 'elements' – hoodies, neets (a new New Labour acronym: 'not in employment, education or training') and others who wear their piercings and anti-social behaviour orders with intimidatory swagger. It is the sort of park shelter that suggests something untoward is going on in one of its compartments even when there isn't (although there usually is).

At the shelter they can go one of two ways along the perimeter path around the lake. Turning right will immediately bring them to the cantonment of anglers with their maggot banks and igloo tents and support group of recreational distance-spitters and Stella-swiggers. One of the reasons Mrs Thatcher's love affair with the gated community in Dulwich was so short-lived was that the route to and from it took her through Brixton. They take the narrow path to the left of the shelter – I can see the rim of a bicycle wheel and the toe of a brand-new, fat-laced white trainer poking out of the shadowy alcove closest to where they are walking – without drawing a flicker of interest from the 'elements', who are either shut off with their fishing rods behind their big umbrellas or too locked into their own deals and interests to notice. They just want to be in a place where they have the world behind them, and before them nothing but emptiness.

And so we go along, the five of us, not twenty feet apart. And then, a further twenty feet beyond Mrs Thatcher and her minders, I see Aitch in his broad-brimmed Australian Driza-Bone hat, dog leads cabled round his neck, waiting to pick up after a miniature Schnauzer that is squatting on a greasy, churned-up square of grass.

Aitch seems enviably unfazed by his encounters with Mrs T. 'Saw ole Maggie yesterday,' he might volunteer. 'Looks more like her Spittin' Image every day.' (Or, 'Saw that idiot Geldof': the two of them have been evil-eyeing each other in a feud that dates back many years and involves Geldof accusing Aitch of not keeping his dogs under control around his small daughters, Peaches and the other one, who these days are never out of the papers.)

Aitch touches the brim of his hat in acknowledgement to the advance detective, who assumes a surveillance position, waiting for the others to catch up. He knows Aitch, knows he can be trusted to maintain a neither hostile nor over-chummy neutrality. He doesn't know me. His expression seems to invite an explanation. I tell him I'm waiting for my dog who has found some interesting smells a little way back, to find me. ('Reading his wee-mails,' I think of saying, parroting a woman with a wire-hair Parson Jack Russell, but don't.)

Standing there, the two of us slightly apart from the detective, who is separate from the main group of Mrs Thatcher and her carer companion and his fellow protection officer, in this slightly unreal situation (we know that under their roomy double-breasted navy blue coats both men are armed) Aitch suddenly opens up in a way that has never happened in the years we have been passing the time of day with each other.

I know he has a son, grown up and living in Australia (which may explain his fondness for the slightly ludicrous-looking waxed cotton hat, the kind that has wine corks dangling from it in cartoons). But now he is speaking for the first time of a girlfriend, which makes me adjust my perception of him as a loner, somebody who loves the park, which he has been using since he was a boy (he remembers it in the early post-war years when it was still divided into allotment gardens, his mother coming over to pull a lettuce, some carrots), and notices the seasons; somebody who vegges out at night with a ready-meal and tins of beer that he collapses with his fist and allows to lie where they fall. (Somebody like James, in fact, who I know takes a drink, but whose midden of a flat mysteriously didn't seem to contain any tell-tale cans or bottles when it was ransacked by Kim and Aggie.)

'I took my girlfriend for a meal in the West End on Friday night,' Aitch says. 'And it was deserted, like a walk in a country lane.'

I had passed the precise spot where the bomb was, the piece of pavement where they had parked the car packed with petrol and liquid propane or butane and nails, dozens, probably hundreds of times, without noticing. 'Tiger Tiger'. It meant nothing.

There's a club in Shaftesbury Avenue, close to Piccadilly, part of the soaked concrete Trocadero development, where there's always a queue along the pavement at a certain time of night with the black bouncers with their zephyr earpieces and padded satin bomber jackets and stylish kids with their pants hanging off and the white iPod wires like in the bus-stop posters against their black skin, whose eyes you sometimes lock with and feel old, going home on the bus, take the dog around the block, get the pillows set right for the asthma.

But 'Tiger Tiger'? Nothing. London's Tiger Tiger is one of a national chain of nine late-night venues owned by Novus Leisure, I read in the paper. Tiger Tigers, the report continued, are particularly popular with women and also appeal to older partygoers because of a policy of allowing customers to pre-book booths, removing any chance of having to queue in the cold.

In future of course it will be impossible to sit on the top on the number 19, gazing out of the tagged, hazed window, catching the effervescent blue of the digitised sign on the side of the bus occasionally bubbling up against shop-window displays and stretches of marble curtain-walling, or interacting interestingly with the vivid orange of the Tiger Tiger illuminated sign, tone-on-tone volumetric illusions, a heightened surface complexity, the new optical solids, and not think: 60 litres of petrol found on the back seat and in the boot with a mobile phone trigger; nails strewn around. The first explosion would rupture the gas canisters and produce a fine cloud of gas, petrol and air; a second explosion would then detonate the vapour. That would give you an explosion of the sort the Americans used to flatten the trees in Vietnam, said Sidney Alford, an explosives expert.

Difficult in future to swing right off the Haymarket along Jermyn Street in the direction of St James's, within a few feet of where the metallic green Mercedes was parked, and see the smokers who now throng the pavement outside Tiger Tiger, hugging themselves with their pale bare arms, corralled behind velvet ropes, shifting from foot to foot (the bombers beat the smoking ban by two days), and not think: carnage and deep-body laceration and major head trauma; bodies ruined by nails and glass, torn up. Hard not to gauge how many of them are wearing glasses and recall that the sight of many of the survivors of the London suicide bombings on 7/7 was saved by the glasses they were wearing.

'The new wars' is how they are coming to be referred to in academic circles. Kosovo, Iraq, Afghanistan, but also the wars here. (Although the new prime minister has committed himself to desist from using the Blair–Bush all-purpose rallying-cry, 'the war against terror'.) 'New-Wars Theory and Sources of Insecurity' is a course that has been made available at some British universities. 'Risk Sociology' and 'Terrorism Studies' have also been proving popular in the years since 9/11, particularly with students from overseas.

Khaled Meshaal. Ismail Haniyeh. Fawzi Barhoum. Abdul Rashid Gazi. Jaish al-Islam. The Tawhid and Jihad Brigades. Mumtaz Dogmush. The Popular Resistance Committees . . . Are these among the names and organisations Mrs Thatcher has highlighted or put exclamation marks against over breakfast this morning? They all appear in a single piece in a single paper, an article about the BBC journalist taken hostage in the Gaza Strip on the 12 March. Already it is day 113. (Day 61 for Madeleine. Day 06 for the new administration of Gordon Brown. In four days it will be 07.07.07 – 'Triple Seven' – an apparently propitious date for Western culture: many thousands of marriages have been planned for that date. There will be a mass wedding ceremony at 7 p.m. on Triple Seven Saturday at Caesars Palace in Las Vegas. Catholics and Charismatic Evangelicals in the US are holding mass rallies.)

A video released to Al Jazeera television two Sundays ago showed the captured BBC correspondent wearing what he said was an explosives vest; the kind of vest that one of the Islamist terrorists in the burning jeep that rammed Glasgow airport apparently had strapped to him. But, even as I stand batting the breeze with Aitch, and Mrs T makes her slow approach along the railing by the lake towards us, Palestinian militias are preparing to liberate Alan Johnston from the rival al-Qaida-inspired faction who have been holding him: dozens of Hamas gunmen in black masks are occupying the rooftops of high-rise apartment blocks that overlook the stronghold of the Dogmush family in the Sabra district of Gaza City. There has been sporadic shooting throughout the morning, with one passer-by shot dead in crossfire. People are burning tyres to drive away mosquitoes and flies. Does she know this?

The 'country lane' effect, as Aitch has described the unusual quiet that took hold in the West End in the wake of the attempted car-bomb attacks on the Haymarket – restaurants deserted, pubs slack, cinemas and theatres closed, only the voices of the military and yellow-reflector-vested members of the emergency services occasionally ripping through the silence – reminded me of something I had read about the new wars in Afghanistan and elsewhere: that the landmines strewn around were difficult to see because they were green and disappeared in the grass.

There has been speculation that the latest bombers are probably British-born but working under the instruction of key al-Qaida figures located in camps in North Waziristan, the tribal land on the Afghan-Pakistan border, high and cold and exposed to flailing wind. The roads there, it is reported, are given over to highwaymen who demand tolls and sometimes abduct children when money is insufficient. Drug gangs and transport mafia dominate the barren economy. The cities have been pounded so hard they are disaggregated into piles of bricks and stones. This is the landscape of the broadcast news, and the novels of the new medieval future: *everything paling away into the murk. The soft ash blowing in loose swirls over the blacktop. Along the shore a burden of dead reeds.* Terminal landscapes. Wasted terrain. Osama – the Lion – called the place Maasada, the Lion's Den.

When Mrs Thatcher and her companions eventually got to where Aitch and I were standing – she cast a curious purse-lipped look Aitch's way, gave a half-nod and blinked rapidly several times – they opted for the path that leads away from the lake and follows the curve of the D-shape that defines the sub-tropical garden. Usually at this time of the year the garden would be filled with people in shorts and bikinis: the looped metal fence which surrounds it is useful for families with young children, while the dense shelter belt of shrubs and trees, planted in raised beds to create the mild micro-climate in which yucca and banana plants thrive, provides the sunbathers with natural screens that they use to protect their privacy.

But the garden is dripping and deserted. During the winter months the more vulnerable species are shrouded in fleece and straw and protective white plastic whose twine ties, spaced at head, waist and feet levels, inevitably suggest a trussed-up body shape, or body bags. (Although it has never occurred to me before, I am reminded now of the television pictures of Mrs Tebbit, wife of Margaret Thatcher's trusted Rottweiler figure, Norman, being lowered down the face of the Grand Hotel in Brighton after the IRA bomb went off during the Conservative conference of 1984. The entire front of the building had been blown out by the force of the blast. Mrs Tebbit was strapped to a stretcher and being lowered vertically past gouts of water erupting from ruptured pipes and rooms whose furnishings and personal belongings – flower-patterned quilts, wall lamps hanging by the wires but somehow still burning – were clearly visible. Mrs Thatcher, it would later emerge, was at that very moment letting it be known she wanted Marks and Spencer to open immediately so that delegates, many of them forced to flee wearing only carpet slippers and dressing-gowns, could replace clothes lost in the explosion.)

As she proceeds around the perimeter of the garden, Mrs T stops every so often to reach up to a drooping branch or out to a flabby rosette of leaves to apparently express her concern about how they are being affected by the weather. And it is only now I notice something that should have been obvious from the beginning: no handbag. She is without the item which came to symbolise her legendary bossiness and indomitability and which she turned into a verb: to handbag, or (more commonly) to be handbagged. She isn't carrying one of the bucket-sized handbags which became part of her armoury. 'Margaret Thatcher carried the authority of her office always with her. It was in her handbag,' Douglas Hurd, her Northern Ireland, Home and Foreign Secretary at various times, once said. 'She was asserting it the whole time'.

Even in the famous picture of her standing in the gun turret of a Saracen tank, taken after the Falklands, kitted out in hooded headscarf and fly-eye desert goggles, she has a handbag over her arm.

What is remembered in the body is well remembered. The presence of learned culture in the body, wrote Elaine Scarry, must at least in part be seen as originating in the body, attributed to the refusal of the body to disown its own early circumstances, its mute and often beautiful insistence on absorbing into its rhythms and postures the signs that it inhabits a particular space at a particular time.

It is said that within a few months of life British infants have learned to hold their eyebrows in a raised position. And a muscle memory keeps sending Mrs Thatcher's pale, manicured right hand with its prominent wrist-bone and thin blue veins travelling along her other arm in an attempt to push the slipping strap – which of course isn't there – back towards the clamp of her elbow.

In a similarly reflexive action, her carer's hand constantly reaches out and hovers around the small of Mrs Thatcher's back. It is noticeable, though, that, no matter how many times this happens, her fingers never make actual contact with the nap of the camel-hair coat nearly identical to her own. The women are of similar height, build and general demeanour. But for this business with the hands, anybody watching from a distance, through a hair-trigger zoom or with the naked eye, would find it difficult telling the two of them apart.

It is often said that today's abundance of media images creates a screen between the individual and the world, and that this is the source of the feeling we all increasingly have of seeing everything but of being able to do nothing. The media gives us images of everything – but only images.

He had only realised Kate Middleton lived a street away, and had been living there for two or three years, when some houses that came up on the TV news looked naggingly familiar. The houses were the backdrop to pictures of the paparazzi climbing over each other to squeeze off shots of Prince William's girlfriend as she left home for work in the morning.

Kate Middleton had started 2007, according to Princess Diana's private secretary, Patrick Jephson, writing in the *Spectator*, with the year 'stretching ahead of her like an enchanted garden'. Prince William was going to announce their engagement and she therefore would be in line to become Queen. But after a series of highly publicised paparazzi chases ominously like the one which resulted in the death of his mother, the prince announced that he and Miss Middleton had agreed, after several years as a couple, to go their separate ways. Nevertheless rumours persisted in the press about them 'spending secret nights together' out of the media spotlight. And on Monday all the papers had run pictures of Kate Middleton sitting in the row behind Prince William at the concert held to mark the tenth anniversary of his mother's death, singing along (so they said, and the event had been televised) to Take That's 'I Want You Back (For Good)'.

After registering where she lived, he had sometimes noticed the snappers lurking in their cars in the street, which was very 'old Chelsea' and narrow and popular with motorbike couriers and taxis as a rat-run to the river (and treacherous because of that). They sometimes rested their coffee cartons on the roofs of each other's cars as they stood around chatting; the cartons lay in the gutter after they had gone: the observers observed. He had never seen the girl, though. And then that Tuesday – the same Tuesday he had once more spotted Mrs Thatcher turning about the park – he had almost charged into Kate Middleton in the nearest Tesco Local on the King's Road. It had been both their faults and they had mumbled apologies to each other: he had been going the wrong way, backtracking, against the after-work traffic, and she had been going too fast with her eyes fixed on the floor.

She was tall; he only came up to her chin; and she had her hair scraped back in a pony-tail instead of the usual loose way she wore it in public, so he hadn't been one hundred per cent sure at first. But there were pictures of her taken at Wembley at the weekend – *Wills' Kate*, as she was described – on the covers of one or two of the freshly delivered gossip weeklies on display in the small periodicals section in the 'Household Cleaners and Detergents' aisle, and a quick check against them confirmed that he was right.

What he hadn't expected was to come face to face with her again while he was doing this. But if she had any recollection of ever seeing him before in her life, she didn't let on. She was wearing tight white jeans of the type routinely referred to as 'spray-on' in these very magazines, and the tightness meant she had to lower herself, bending from the knees, to pick up a copy of the evening paper which was stacked on the lowest shelf. She added it to a basket which already contained breakfast cereal and a two-pack of kitchen rolls.

As she no doubt already knew, there was a colour snap of her on page fifteen, taken at the previous day's Wimbledon. Her mouth was open in a squeal, cheering on the Spaniard, Rafael Nadal, in his third-round match on the Centre Court. But the couple in the row behind were sharing a tartan blanket draped over their knees, emulating her future in-laws who insist on a rug in the state Bentley when they are out performing royal duties in weather only slightly less than ideal. It gave a doleful aspect to the picture – a blanket in July – but also by suggesting that codgerdom, the only end of stultifying protocol, could only be a matter of a state wedding away.

There was a woman at the next till – early twenties, blonde, bad skin, high colour in her face – who he was starting to suspect was probably bulimic. (He was hoping for a glimpse of her teeth. Doesn't the acid in the vomit start to strip the enamel away after a while?) At first she had just the two items: a small sliced white batch loaf and a family-size packet of Minstrels, plus a slippery stack of *New!*, *Now*, *Star* and other junk magazines. But then she had reached down to the display below the counter, put there to encourage impulse buys except that hers were clearly well-rehearsed and premeditated, and picked out two Turkish Delights, one milk, one plain, and then a third. And then – this as if as an afterthought, when the other items had already been scanned and bagged by the assistant – a Ripple, a box of Maltesers and two tubes of After Eight. A single-queue system was in operation for the multiple check-outs. And she glanced anxiously behind her before sliding a Galaxy, a chocolate-orange bar and a fourth Turkish Delight across the counter, covered by her hand.

So immersed was he in the details of this innocent but potentially sordid transaction – the basement living room, the gorging, the trips to the bathroom, back to *New!* and *EastEnders*; a woman scoring her drug of choice at the local Tesco – that he failed to react when the man who had been serving him – he was a handsome African called 'Tevo', according to his ID badge – raised his hand and impatiently beckoned the next customer.

By the time he bent to pick up his second bag – it was the one with the bottles – he found it trapped behind the legs with the white spray-on jeans, bunched at the ankles and pleated behind the knees. With a smile which in the years ahead she would no doubt come to bestow on Aids

31

patients and cheering crowds lining the streets of Papua, New Guinea and good souls who have offered retired guide dogs a final home, she reached down and swung the bag over at him (she knew very well by now he had clocked her) with a clink.

A couple of minutes later she followed him through the automatic doors, and that's when the fun really started.

What had been an ordinary evening street scene of shoppers and buses, the alkie with his dog squatted by the cashpoint, the phoners and texters, the smokers loitering outside the Louisiana rib-shack, the Lebanese juice-bar, the traditional pub recently turned into a branch of Babushka, all Tesco's near-neighbours, became all at once a phantasmagoria.

It was like Kate Middleton's appearance on the street was the cue for special effects to turn the rain machine on, for the music to be brought up high and the smokers, taciturn and sullen to that point, to become animated into a jostling crowd scene.

The big glass door slid open, and she emerged, and it was like the opening sequence of a high-end video with the tracking shots and the overhead cranes, or a musicalised play by Dennis Potter where the heroine opens her mouth and sings in the rumbling Negro baritone of the Deep River Boys, and the beggar throws off his tattered blanket and stumblebum drunkenness and hoofs it through one of the more challenging routines of Fred Astaire or Gene Kelly.

The skies opened and the hail hammered down. There

32

was a soundtrack, and it was provided by some kids in a car pumping out the hit of the summer which, as luck would have it, was called 'Umbrella' by Rihanna (feat. Jay-Z), which had apparently started a craze around the clubs for smuggling in collapsible umbrellas that were suddenly raised and whirled around the dance floor, Gene Kelly fashion, whenever the song by Rihanna (feat. Jay-Z) came on.

So it was July and it was like *Singin' in the Rain* and it was also like the scene at the end of *White Christmas* when Bing and Danny Kaye and all the cast gather round the tree to sing the title song while snow softly gusts in from the street at the back of the stage.

Except the hailstones hurt. They were big and saw-edged and could cause minor abrasions to bald heads.

The man petting the dog belonging to the guy bedded down beside the money hole-in-the-wall turned out to be a pap, who leapt into action the minute his target appeared. And then a second snapper emerged from the door to the cinema, and a third and fourth from the entrance to the pizza restaurant, while others kerb-crawled alongside her in cars and on motorbikes, the ice-balls ricocheting crazily off the Zuni-beetle shells of their big phallic Leicas and the semi-spherical peaks of their truckers' caps and their windscreens, and seemed oblivious to members of the public yelling at them to *leave the girl alone!*

There are really two kinds of life, notes the American writer James Salter. There is the one people believe you are living, and there is the other. It is this other which causes the trouble, this other we long to see.

Chapter Two

Click to create a shrine. Unlike a gravestone, these tributes will not weather over the years.

Abukar Mohammed
1991 to 2007
Aged: 16
From: Stockwell

```
        * + * JUST * + .
      + . . * + . + * . * +
      * . + *SPRINKLIN.* + .
      + . . * + . + * . * + .
    + , *YOUR. + * PAGE+ *
    + . . * + . + * . * + .*
      . * * + . * WITH.* .
    + . SOME. * + * * . + * .
        . * + * * + . *+ *
  + ..LOVE.. * + . +GOD BLESS XXX
```

Micki (Mummy of Kylie Whyte-Reynolds, daughter

34

of Terry Embra) 26th Jul 2007 RIP teen angel –
When will this all stop? My thoughts are with your
devastated family. May you have eternal peace xx

Josh R.I.P. 27th Jul 2007
Another young life taken off da streets . . .
XXXXXR.I.P Abuka babes, lyf aint guna b da same
wivout uXXXXX Another young life gone just like
that another family in bits

Gone but definitely not 4gotten.
Raegz from Gipsy Hill. Relation: Friend. 28th Jul
2007 I hadn't seen u 4 long brudda but wen i heard
wat went down i used mind ova matter 2 stop
myself sheddin' tears. aint even known u 4 dat long
only since i started Stockwell Park in yr11. U woz kul
doe fam and itza 100% guarantee i wont 4get man.
Dun NO!!. Inshallah Allah will open up the gates of
paradise for u brudda . . .

Abukar Mohammed was murdered in Stockwell in south
London on the night of 26 July. His family was originally
from Somalia, and he was shot dead at point-blank range
in a random 'execution' after he was chased across the
Stockwell Gardens estate by a gang of teenagers on bikes,
wearing clothes with 'SW9' written on the front, and 'Hot
Spot', their name for the estate, a favourite with drug deal-
ers, on the back.

Abukar was sixteen and he was the tenth young victim

of gun and knife crime in London in six months. In common with all the others, from Michael Dosunmu, age fifteen, shot dead at home in Peckham in early February, to Mark Dinnegan, age fourteen, stabbed in Islington after being chased by a gang of youths at the end of June, Abukar had had a virtual shrine set up in his memory on gonetoosoon.co.uk within just a few hours of word of his murder getting round.

In the early hours of 4 May, with police and volunteers searching the beach and the narrow streets of Praia da Luz, the McCanns' friends and family back in England started to circulate a text message urging everyone '2 light a candle 4 madeleine who was abducted from portugal. we r trying 2 make it a worldwide thing so if u cn plz join in by textin or emailin as many people as u cn'.

Twelve days later the official findmadeleine website was launched. It drew on the expertise of some of Kate and Gerry's friends in broadcasting and the New Media. It featured many pictures of Madeleine taken over the six days of her holiday; the earliest showed her climbing the steps of the EasyJet at East Midlands airport just before she tripped and cut her knee. Also included were casual, intimate snapshots from the family album, innocent and ordinary.

Madeleine's eyes had been stylised into media emblems, the defect in her right eye simplified into an easily recognisable logo.

findmadeleine.com recorded more than 70 million visits in the first three days, and 7,500 messages of support, the last folk ritual of social gathering. That volume of traffic was irresistible to typosquatters who, simply by launching near-name sites with only a single letter difference, could send Madeleine well-wishers and the surfers of second-hand non-experience to porn sites and other sites hastily set up by conmen.

Only eight days after her disappearance, an appeal in the form of a rap entitled 'For The Safe Return Of The Little Toddler To Her Family', appeared on YouTube:

> 8 days gone since this lil girl was snatched
> people praying all over just bring her back
> can you imagine how it feels to be her mum and dad
> or her little brother and sister who wont understand
> 3 years old i ask my self why the world is so cold
> but we must keep the faith and not let this go
> together we will find maddie dont give up hope
> its times like these we hold our family near
> the public is there only hope to make her reappear
> i see this on the news and i want to shed a tear
> this is the truth this is a fuked up world
> who could do that to a precious little girl
> its just not right madeleine mccann deserves to have a life
> with her family where she should be
> if youve got her give her back im beggin you please
> stop putting her family through all this grief
> its her birthday tomorrow what better present could there be
> than setting her free
> just let her be

The voice sounded like the voice of a child. Clicking on the singer's Profile, though, brought up the picture of a balding man in his late twenties sitting in what looked like a bedsit with a cheap boxwood guitar.

Given the unlimited opportunities which the media landscape now offers to the wayward imagination, wrote J. G. Ballard, I feel we should immerse ourselves in the most destructive element, ourselves, and swim.

There is a view of photography as being something 'that seizes a moment in life and is its death', and the photo gallery on the Madeleine site could be offered as proof of that. Some took the view that the sheer volume of pictures in existence showed that the parents hadn't wanted to experience their daughter as a person so much as record her having the experiences they were fortunate enough to be able to buy.

But could it be that the McCanns wanted their daughter to become as familiar to strangers through her image as she was to them, so that they, too, would wake in the morning and – before they could locate it – might feel that there was now a tragic absence in their own lives; something catastrophic that in their first moments of waking they were having trouble remembering?

The media of real life. The murder leisure industry.

Privacy is so last century, the headline read, but we need help to adjust.

Chapter Three

Myrobella, the Blairs' constituency home at Trimdon Colliery, was once the big house of the village, occupied by the doctor's family, solid and detached among all the encroaching narrow terraces of pitmen's houses. It stands in full view, but it isn't easy to find.

From near the top of the hill that leads from one of the Trimdons to another – Trimdon Colliery up to Trimdon Grange, which eventually connects to a third Trimdon, the Village where the church that provided the setting for Blair's coming-of-age 'people's princess' speech can be found and, only a little way up the hill from there, Trimdon Labour Club, the place where he launched his campaign to become leader of the Party in 1994 and announced his intention of standing down as prime minister thirteen years later, a modest, modern building he thinks of as his 'spiritual home' – gazing back across the scrub meadows with their punctuation points of brown shaggy-backed horses indolently cropping, and irregular grassed-over depressions where the coal seams once ran, is a dense copse with a mossy Victorian slate roof poking out of the top of it. This is Myrobella, the house the Blairs bought in 1984, the year after he was elected MP for Sedgefield in County Durham.

But the closer you get to it, coming down the hill past the miners' welfare cottages with their barbered lawns and recently constructed cubistic, architecturally adventurous hard-edged glass porches, past the terraces with their uniform vertical swivel-blinds and elderly men gardening in their vests, hard muscle turned soft, the harder the Blair house is to see.

When the pits were working, Trimdon Colliery, like all the neighbouring colliery villages, would have been a dirty place. The original owners of Myrobella (stove-hatted Myron, pin-curled and pinafored Bella?) would have looked out over a landscape of pit-heads and winding gear permanently slaked with the heavy industrial fallout of soot and ferrous pollutants and dust. The bricks of the original terraces are still nearly as black as muck.

The modern world – the post-Thatcher world – has announced its arrival with a lot of white. The timber of the old front doors has been stripped out and replaced with waxy white PVC; the windows are white plastic and the 'nets' put up at them are also white with occasional lime-green or bubblegum pink detailing.

The front of Guappo's barber's shop which stands in a sort of fork in the road shortly before the main rundown shopping street in Trimdon Colliery – the sign outside says 'Hair design for men' – is jazzily black-and-white and has nothing about it to indicate that it is the near-neighbour of the big house where, until recently, the prime minister lived.

Myrobella is approached along an uneven narrow track with a terrace of half a dozen miners' houses running down one side. The police have taken over the house nearest the Blairs. There is a heavy round-the-clock police presence and a series of barriers ringing Myrobella. There is a wooden barrier with an urgent caution notice on it and then a brick gate-house where evidence of some of the duty officers' home comforts – a radio, some washing-up liquid, an electric kettle – can be glimpsed through a window. Police armed with sniper rifles patrol the perimeter. The house itself has been screened from the public with close-planted perennials and tall box hedges, creating a dark and rather oppressive atmosphere. This is amplified by the dank patch of municipal playground full of nursery-coloured rides and brimming with deadly negative potential – the inch-thick subaudible rubber tiling squelches underfoot – that has been carved out of quarter of an acre of what was originally Myrobella's either front or back garden.

The uncertainty arises from the fact that none of the house's doors, certainly none of its windows, is visible. The process of concealment has been so well achieved that all Myrobella's particulars – homeliness, openness, availability of natural light, original features, true wear and tear, stability, renovations, orientation, everything about the house – is subject to speculation, and has to be guessed at rather than known. Many people would argue that in these respects, Myrobella is emblematic of Blair himself, 'the man with no shadow': a formidable building that appears, no matter how many times you circle it, to have no doors.

In the early years, before the era of 'celebrity government' had been inaugurated under Tony Blair as prime minister, he used to hold his regular Saturday-morning surgeries at the house. There would be complaints towards the end that it was impossible to get in to see him; that the nearest you ever got was his Sedgefield agent, John Burton, and that Blair himself didn't know the full name of anybody in the village. Even in his years as a fledgling MP, though, from 1983 on, for somebody committed to simple Christian principles of charity, equality and good intentions as Blair was, his receiving of constituents at Myrobella on Saturdays must have had something uncomfortably Thomas Hardy-like about it: a tableau of the halt and the poor huddled against the rain and the biting wind, carrying their problems to the grand house.

(No telling of the tale of Gordon Brown can be complete without reference to his standing as a 'son of the manse' and the effect it had on him as a boy growing up in a house which was often the place of last resort for many of his father's hard-up Kirkcaldy parishioners. Dr Brown, who was considered a saintly man, believed it was his duty to help feed, clothe and encourage those at the bottom of the heap. 'Living in a manse,' Gordon Brown later said, 'you find out quickly about life and death and the meaning of poverty, injustice and unemployment.')

Just before the barber shop on the road that leads down into Trimdon Village, visitors are given a subtle clue that they could be within striking distance of the former prime minister's house. 'Premier Court', a sign announces at the entrance to a new cul-de-sac development of what the brochures generally describe as 'executive homes'. The cul-de-sac of double-fronted, pale brick houses where Kate and Gerry McCann live with their children a few miles north of Leicester looks similar in the pictures. The difference is that Orchard House in the commuter village of Rothley is a close neighbour of The Ridgeway, singled out as one of the ten most expensive places to live in Britain by the *Sunday Times* at around the time of Madeleine's disappearance.

Five miles to the north of Trimdon are the former mining communities of Haswell and Haswell Plough where the (at that stage still anonymous) Labour donor David Abrahams made a killing in 2001, when he put together parcels of land occupied by disused buildings and obtained planning permission so that the sites could be sold on for residential development.

Trimdon and Kelloe pit at Haswell were once linked underground. Pairs of hewers drove roadways into the coal, fifteen feet wide, and the subterranean road between Trimdon and Kelloe stretched for mile after mile, with new roadways struck off to the left and right at intervals of twenty yards. The two pits are connected in local folklore by the Trimdon Disaster of 1882 in which seventy-four people were killed. But, whereas Haswell has become a popular commuter village built by Miller Homes,

Trimdon itself remains a property black spot, stubbornly unarbitrageable and apparently ignored in the rush to coalfield regeneration.

North Moor Avenue contains only a handful of closed or failing businesses. The Grey Horse is closed down and slowly collapsing. Inside the Royal, Blair's local if he had one, it is like a permanent rainy Tuesday in late autumn. An overfed Staffie waddles up to the bar, sniffs each arriving customer's shins, waddles back to his place in front of the fire trailing a thread of shining drool and a pungent body odour. Portrait of an English summer.

And now Myrobella, whose comings and goings were some of the few signs of life in Trimdon Colliery, is starting to give the appearance of being uninhabited, maybe even abandoned in spite of the outgoing PM's expressions of deep sentimental attachment and pledges of lifelong fealty. A van came and collected many of the Blairs' personal belongings a few days after his valedictory address to the House of Commons. Already the uniformed officers who have been assigned to the house for ten years seem listless, even apprehensive. They are standing watch over an absence. They are guarding nothing. They are bearing witness to a kind of voluntary self-erasure.

A week after Blair left office, the viewers of *Richard and Judy* voted as their YouTube clip of the week a little girl Madeleine's age – a little girl very like Madeleine – refusing to eat her breakfast and sobbing over the void left in her life by the disappearance of Tony Blair. *I love Tony Bair!* she wails. *I want Tony Bair!* Doesn't she like the new prime minister? her mother asks from behind the camera, knowing the answer, pushing her daughter's buttons, prompting her bleatings for the benefit of the YouTube audience. *Noooooo! Wheeeere is he?* She bangs the table with her spoon and screams even louder. *I love Tony Bair!* ('Thousands of little girls want him to be president so they can have him on the TV screen and run their fingers through the image of his hair.' This from a political commentator in the Sixties, on the subject of Bobby Kennedy. 'Nonchalance is the key word,' the writer added. 'Carefully studied nonchalance. The harder a man tries, the better he must hide it. Style becomes substance.')

Blair's vanishing act when it happened, happened quickly. There were big attention-grabbing events: back-to-back, piled-up catastrophes and near-catastrophes – the terrorist attacks, the floods, foot-and-mouth – and somebody else taking charge of them, doing the reassuring. One minute Blair was part of the national static, and the next he was gone. The fact it had been a long time coming didn't make any difference. The little girl (and, here, it is difficult not to hear David Beckham's voice on his television appeal for information about Madeleine: *Anybody who may have seen this littoo gel . . .*, holding up a picture captioned with the single word *DESAPARECIDA*, the broad diamond-encrusted ring, the buffed pearl-cuticled nails, the big fuck-off watch), the little girl was right. His disappearance from public life was eerie, its stage management both calculated and, in its eventual effects, its tiny but tangible tipping of the world (that trailing sleeve gathering up the dirt of King's Cross station, Cherie's parting shot of 'We won't miss you!' to the world's press gathered outside Number 10, the look that said 'Zip it!' that he shot her) unexpectedly unsettling.

Blair had announced his departure from public life at Trimdon Labour Club on 10 May. It was a full-scale media event, with satellite trucks crowding the village and reporters doing pieces to camera all along the edge of the green. The New Labour anthems – 'Search for the Hero Inside Yourself' and 'Things Can Only Get Better' – were sprayed around, and people appeared with placards, some (as observers noted) in suspiciously similar styles: '10 Years, 3 Elections, 1 Great Britain'; 'Britain Says Thanks', 'Tony Rocks'.

His bowing-out coincided with another, more subliminal subtraction: it was the last weekend of the football season, with the switching of rhythms in all English towns and cities, the adjusting of habits and routines, of traffic-flow systems and shop opening hours that the close-season always means. The football grounds falling silent is experienced, even by people who have never set foot in them and maybe resent the disruption that match days bring, not so much as an absence as a lack of presence: the very traces of life extinguished, of death stalking through the centre of life.

Before their final game of the season against Chelsea in London on 13 May, Everton players wore Madeleine T-shirts during the warm-up. Brian Healy, her grandfather, was a lifelong supporter of the team that is traditionally followed by Catholics in Liverpool, and soon the family would release a picture of Madeleine wearing her blue 'Toffees' shirt. It was piercingly reminiscent of Holly Wells and Jessica Chapman photographed in their red-and-white Beckham tops just hours before they were murdered by Ian Huntley in Soham. And just two games into the 2007–8 football season in mid-August, an eleven-year-old, Rhys Jones, died when he was hit in the head by a bullet fired by a hooded figure on a mountain bike while he was on his way home from football practice in the Croxteth area of Liverpool. Rhys Jones too was an Evertonian. And three days after his murder, pictures of Rhys in his Everton jersey were being flashed onto the big screens at Goodison Park alongside the continuing appeals for information about the disappearance of Madeleine showing close-ups of the defect in her eye and the photograph of her in her Everton top.

The observance of a minute's silence had become a regular feature of match days at Goodison over the previous twelve months, as Evertonians in the armed forces continued to be casualties of the wars in Iraq and Afghanistan. On the first Sunday after his murder, there was a minute's applause for Rhys Jones before Everton v. Blackburn, and his favourite tune, 'Johnny Todd', the *Z-Cars* theme and Everton anthem, was played. The following morning the Everton coach stopped on the way to training so that the players could add signed football boots and jerseys and a signed ball to the shrine that had been made in the pub car park where Rhys died.

Within forty-eight hours of his murder, Steve and Melanie Jones, Rhys's parents, had submitted to the harrowing ordeal of a televised interview with Richard Bilton, the soft-spoken BBC reporter who had been covering the McCann case from Portugal and had interviewed Kate and Gerry McCann in their apartment in Praia da Luz. And the Joneses, along with their older son, Owen, all wearing scarves and the Everton colours, were standing at the side of the pitch to join in the minute's applause on 25 August, weeping, of course, their faces reddened and smeared, their hair and clothes dishevelled, looking wrung-out with exhaustion and grief. Looking how people are expected to look when the comfortable facade of life has been torn away as a result of the unimaginable happening. The Joneses looked, in other words, the way Kate and Gerry McCann – controlled, collected, articulate, focused – had stubbornly refused to in all their appearances in public since Madeleine had gone missing.

Gerry McCann was a heart specialist at the Glenfield Hospital in Leicester. But it was his background in sports medicine which had opened doors to the likes of David Beckham and Alex Ferguson and Manchester United's Portuguese winger, Cristiano Ronaldo. Both teams at Celtic's home game against Aberdeen on the last day of the Scottish season had worn yellow armbands to mark Madeleine's fourth birthday. Four days later, on 16 May, Gerry's brother John, accompanied by the former England rugby captain Martin Johnson, had launched the official fundraising website dedicated to Madeleine, and the same day his sister Philomena – 'Auntie Phil' – had travelled from her home in Glasgow to meet the prime minister-in-waiting, Gordon Brown, in his office at the House of Commons; the 'Iron Chancellor' had apparently shed a tear as he held her hand.

Gerry McCann and Kate Healy were clever children from working-class backgrounds, in Glasgow and Liverpool respectively. Both their fathers earned their livings manually, as joiners, and they had both aspired to become, and after the long slog of study had eventually qualified as, doctors. Much of the hostility directed towards them from the early days of the search for their daughter seemed to stem from the fact that they had been educated out of their class. Their accents – Gerry's in particular, which was heard most often – connected them to the backgrounds they had grown away from, while their profession was an unmistakeable sign of where they were heading.

In the meantime, in midlife – they were both thirty-nine – they were unrooted; they fitted nowhere. The sports-leisure wear that they wore for photo opportunities in Praia – Kate's ghetto-style trainers, Gerry's cropped trousers – seemed too up-to-the-minute for people who called themselves doctors; the names they had given their daughters – 'Madeleine', with its Proustian resonance; 'Amelie' rather than plain Emily – appeared pretentiously Frenchified and 'European' to people of their parents' generation.

That was one difference between the McCanns and Steve and Melanie Jones: the Joneses were part of a community that they knew and that knew them; they belonged. And their belonging, given vivid expression in the way they were embraced by, first, the Goodison and then the wider Merseyside tribes – the hated 'Johnny Todd', for example, was played at a Liverpool game for the first time in living memory, a few days after their son's murder; the red of Liverpool became as common as the blue of Everton bunted across his shrine – was seen to represent a kind of authenticity that in the McCanns was lacking. By August Kate and Gerry had already emigrated to the new territory established by the likes of Bill Clinton and Oprah Winfrey and Richard Branson, where networking, influence and giving are inextricably intertwined.

Among his friends Gerry McCann enjoyed a reputation as a joker, the fiery centre of any social gathering; his loud Glaswegian accent would come out on those occasions. But the Gerry who presented himself to the television cameras and in the newspapers was the Dr Sobersides (with a certain Roy Keane-like truculence) his tremulous patients were ushered in to see about their arteriosclerosis and pulmonary infarctions and to have angiograms and cardiac ultrasounds and other fearsome procedures initiated. His hand in their chest, working under the rib-cage; Swan-Ganz catheters inside the heart, the pressure transducer at the tip of the catheter, the tube hoovering up the spurting blood.

After a lifetime of regenerating spare parts, the nerve and muscle cells' capacity for rejuvenation gradually shuts down. One after another, cardiac muscle cells cease to live – the heart loses strength.

The maximal rate attainable by a perfectly healthy heart falls by one beat every year. The rapidity of circulation slows down: each heart beat pushes out less blood than it did a year earlier. Perhaps in an attempt to compensate, the blood pressure tends to rise somewhat. One third of people over the age of sixty-five have hypertension.

As the pump ages, its inner lining and valves thicken, calcifications appear in the valves and muscle.

The left ventricle, the most powerful part of the cardiac pump and the source of the muscular strength that nourishes every organ and tissue of the body, is injured in virtually every heart attack – each cigarette, each pat of butter, each slice of meat and each increment of hypertension make the coronary arteries stiffen their resistance to the flow of blood.

Digitalis, morphine, theophylline, ergot, adrenalin, stramomium, terramycin, coramine (the means to jumpstart the heart).

'Irregular squirming' – the terminal condition called ventricular fibrillation, the agonal act of a heart that is becoming reconciled to its eternal rest.

Medicine is the profession most likely to attract people with high personal anxieties about dying.

When the cadaver dogs, two liver-and-white springers – Keela, able to detect minute quantities of blood, and Eddie, trained to detect dead bodies – were flown to

Portugal from Britain at the end of July at the request of the Policia Judiciaria, unverified stories were leaked to the press saying that the dogs had detected traces of Madeleine's blood or bodily fluids on Kate McCann's skirt and on her bible. The claims were dismissed by her friends on the grounds that her job had brought her into contact with half a dozen dead bodies in just the weeks prior to their family holiday starting.

Modern death in tiled hospital rooms, and silent technologised removal. *The greater the scientific advance, the more primitive the fear.*

Football for the spectator represents youth, vitality, community, spontaneity, the universal experience of acquiring a place in the world. Doctors, which both the McCanns are, serve as reminders of our inevitable personal, organic decay.

Something interesting occurred as the weeks and months of Madeleine's disappearance lengthened: Kate McCann's Scouser accent, not much more than an inflection at first, thickened and became what it must have been when she was still being shaped by Liverpool and she was young and being chatted up by Scally youths in the pubs (or maybe already the trendy eateries and health clubs and rugby-club bars).

The coarseness of the accent at times seemed at odds with the smoothness of her skin and purity of her complexion; the still unblotched colour – the mask-like, magazine-model good looks which had been widely commented on and were credited with the blanket coverage the case was being given compared to other previous and already forgotten snatched-child stories.

She had finally become pregnant with Madeleine in late 2002 through IVF, and in 2004 became pregnant again with twins. The McCanns spent that year in Amsterdam, where he was working on new heart-imaging techniques. Back in England they moved into their large house in the upmarket development in Rothley. They had family connections with the village: Kate's uncle, Brian Kennedy, and his wife Janet lived there and the Kennedys were regarded as pillars of the community. In the weeks after the catastrophe in Portugal he took care of Kate and Gerry's house, forwarded mail and fielded questions from local reporters and journalists who had been sent up to do backgrounders and 'colour' pieces in the area.

Many years before, following a series of rapes and violent sexual murders in villages on the other side of Leicester, an American, the LA policeman turned best-selling novelist Joseph Wambaugh, had come to the East Midlands to gather material for a true-crime book called *The Blooding*. With an outsider's eye, Wambaugh had noted 'cottages with bottle-glass leaded windows' and 'tall young villagers passing in and out of cottage doors, in a semi-genuflection', but also that the city of Leicester itself, 'like most of Britain', had acquired a large Asian and East Indian population. 'The people of Leicester have acquired an unfair reputation for being offhand', he wrote. 'Yet it's hard to judge people harshly when they sprinkle their speech with endearments like "m'duck" (it sounds like "midook").'

Wambaugh's primary interest, and the subject of his book, was a scientific discovery that in the mid-Eighties had only just been announced: the technique known as 'genetic fingerprinting'. It was Wambaugh's conviction that DNA testing was going to transform forensic science as much as standard fingerprinting did in the 1890s that had brought him to Leicester University and the lab of the geneticist Alec Jeffreys.

In a fringe project spun off from his main project, which involved a study to determine how genes evolve, Jeffreys had unexpectedly hit upon a method of mapping human genes that produced a DNA image which was individually specific. By showing huge numbers of genetic markers resembling the bar codes used to identify supermarket items, Jeffreys proved that it was possible to positively identify a person using even the tiniest sample of blood or saliva or semen: the only people on the face of the planet with identical DNA would be identical twins. The little circumstances of no two lives anywhere in the world are just alike.

It was an accident of history that a scientific discovery made in their adopted home city twenty years earlier would lead to the McCanns being declared *arguidos* by the Portuguese police. There is also the odd coincidence of the McCanns' friend Dr David Payne, one of the 'Tapas 7' who was having dinner with them on the night Madeleine disappeared, being a senior research fellow at Leicester

University in the laboratories where Sir Alec Jeffreys, enormously wealthy now from the patents he holds, still works.

Media mouthpiece was a new role for Kate McCann's uncle, Brian Kennedy, but not entirely unfamiliar: he was a recently retired headmaster and so used to keeping unruly elements in check. He knew the protocols from many years' exposure to victims' families on the television news, and the questions in the first few weeks tended to be of the human-interest sort and politely reticent rather than probing. (It would take a full month from the disappearance for a German reporter to break rank and ask the McCanns how they felt about the fact that 'more and more people seem[ed] to be pointing the finger' at them, during a press conference in Berlin.)

Brian Kennedy was usually filmed against the war memorial in Rothley where several hundred people, including the new classmates Madeleine was due to join in September, had left soft toys and flowers and tied yellow ribbons to the railings. Nevertheless, in those early days when the story was still breaking, welcome back-up was provided by Esther McVey, a media-savvy schoolfriend of Kate McCann's from Liverpool and another high achiever. In her twenties she had been a presenter for BBC children's television and a talking hair-do on the breakfast show *GMTV* before becoming involved with numerous charities and active in party politics: she was the Conservative Parliamentary candidate for Wirral West in the 2005 General Election. (Justine McGuinness, the McCann family spokesman in Praia da Luz, had fought West Dorset for the Lib Dems in 2005 and come second to the Conservative front-bencher Oliver Letwin.)

By the summer of 2007 Esther McVey was the managing director of her own company Making It (UK) Ltd, as well as the founder of Winning Women, an organisation described on her website as being 'about Fun, Information, Infrastructure and mixing with Influential People, capturing opportunities that come your way in life'. Her biggest scalp and the most impressive IP she had met so far that year, she blogged, was Barack Obama, the man chasing Hillary Clinton for the 2008 Democratic presidential nomination. As somebody who had followed Obama's 'political fairytale' and watched 'his mesmeric performances' on the news, she had jumped at the chance to have lunch with him – 'I flew out at the weekend to meet this political phenomena [sic]' – when an old friend left a message inviting her to meet up in Washington with him 'and a couple of guys'.

'Billy and a couple of guys turned out to be: the chairman of NBC, the publisher of *People* magazine, various senior CEOs of business, all very successful business people and family people, Kelly Rowlands of Destiny's Child who provided us with some beautiful acoustic songs before lunch, myself and Barack Obama!'

Invited to review the papers on Andrew Marr's Sunday morning politics programme on BBC1 some months after becoming one of the seven directors of the fundraising company Find Madeleine: Leaving No Stone Unturned, as well as its official spokesperson, she reprised her Obama encounter: 'He exuded a calm warmth. If he'd been a musician he'd have been a laidback jazz singer – not pop, not punk, but steady and worldly, not singing the blues but he knew what the blues were and wanted a way out of there. He was tall and slim, athletic long-distance-runner physique – no doubt a discipline he'll need in the presidential marathon to come.'

A rumour ran around the online forums and chatrooms for a while that Gerry McCann's father had been a leading light in the Labour party and that this explained his access to Gordon Brown and, through him, to the Browns' good friend in Scotland, J. K. Rowling. Jo Rowling was among a number of public figures who had quickly come forward with offers of rewards totalling two and a half million pounds for information leading to Madeleine's safe return; she also asked booksellers to put up posters of Madeleine when the seventh and last in the Harry Potter series, *Harry Potter and the Deathly Hallows*, went on sale at the climax of a global publicity push at midnight on 21 July.

The chatter and twitter about Gerry McCann's father wasn't true. It was a minor squall in the blizzard of rumour that blew through that summer. But Gerry – somebody used to riding the high of sleep deprivation, dressed day and night in surgical scrubs, banks of beepers on his belt, pockets cluttered with pen-lights, EKG calipers, haemostats, stethoscopes, seven-gauge, seven-inch needles, with a twelve-inch trail of tubing carried casually in its sterile packaging, ready, should he be the first at a cardiac arrest (a CODE BLUE) to slide needle under collarbone and into the great subclavian vein, feeding the serpent tubing down the vena cava in a cathartic ritual that established medical mastery over the human body – Gerry was increasingly featured in the papers 'striding purposefully between meetings with senior politicians and religious leaders, zealously banging the drum for missing children'. To his supporters, he was an inspiring example of somebody who (in the well-known alliterative of the self-help mantra) was turning adversity to advantage, transforming personal tragedy into something positive and finding in his own catastrophe a cause.

Like their friend Esther McVey, it did seem to be the case that Gerry was able to command access to famous and powerful people such as Rowling and Richard Branson and the owner of TopShop, Sir Philip Green, who put his Learjet at the McCanns' disposal for their tour of European capitals in early June.

The appointment of Michael Caplan, QC, and Angus McBride of the fashionable London firm of Kingsley Napley as their legal advisers set tongues wagging and sparked a whole new chain of real and frenziedly Googled-up connections. The results showed that Tony Blair was reported to have contacted Kingsley Napley at the beginning of the year over the threat of arrest in the cash for honours scandal. Other recent high-profile clients included the England football captain, John Terry, over an alleged nightclub brawl, and the self-styled 'rogue trader', the dodgy banker Nick Leeson.

Michael Caplan (described in Chambers legal directory as 'the weapon of choice for battleship cases') was best known for two things: his obsession with secrecy, and for representing the repressive Chilean dictator Pinochet who was arrested just after having tea with his friend Lady Thatcher and faced extradition to Spain. When he was freed on the grounds of his deteriorating health, Caplan personally saw Pinochet onto the plane back to Santiago and made sure the General took with him the inscribed plate that Margaret Thatcher, having made it clear that he was the only person she trusted to carry out her wishes, had placed in Caplan's safekeeping.

The Blairs spent the summer at their friend Sir Cliff Richard's villa in Barbados. Around the time Caplan and McBride were photographed stepping through the front door at Orchard House in Rothley for the first time, Cherie was snapped on the Côte d'Azure with her best new friend, Bono. It was the dog days of the summer, and the Blairs were by then staying as the guests of Bernard Arnault, the billionaire owner of Louis Vuitton, Dior and other luxury brands, on his yacht on the Riviera.

For a long time – for much of the last century, in fact, wrote Richard Schickel – social commentators have been decrying the steady erosion of our old sense of community. In this context, the celebrity community, which has about it aspects of the extended family, offers a kind of compensation. There is a widespread belief that there is a small and seemingly cohesive group of well-known individuals who share close communal ties with one another at the high centre of our public life – ties that are enhanced by the fact that they share the pleasures and problems inherent in their celebrity status, no matter how disparate their routes to that status have been.

'We're normal people,' Kate McCann protested when her family's transition from being unknown to well known, and the perks that come with the transition – a hotline to senior members of the government, for example – were just starting to raise resentments: the first signs of a backlash were beginning to become apparent in eruptions of public volatility and paranoia. 'We don't have amazing contacts or anything, we just have strong friends. Everyone brainstormed and became very creative. They did what they could and if that meant asking well-known faces, celebrities, it was done. They are normal people too. They wanted to help.'

The house, backing on to fields, surrounded by countryside used by the local hunt, so close to the properties the *Sunday Times* had singled out as the most expensive in the East Midlands, their private pools and tennis courts screened behind dark bosks and bushes at street level but clearly visible from the air, downloadable on Flash Earth, zoom in, zoom out, the burglars' bible, was a statement of what they had achieved.

Gerry had spent three weeks building a climbing frame in the long back garden, an expanse of lawn laid by the developers where forested orchard had once stood, all trace of that old part of the village erased, before they left for their holiday in the Algarve. Along with a children's slide, the coloured Jungle Gym frame was just visible in the aerial shots of the McCann home (a term that always sounded more ominous than 'house' when used in captions) that started appearing online and in the papers.

Police began the excavation of bodies from the back garden of a house in the rundown south-coast resort of Margate soon after the McCanns returned from Portugal in early September. And there was a correspondence between the helicopter pictures of the crime scene with its canvas screens and fingertip searches and methodical police activity, and photographs of the McCann house in Rothley, sealed and silent and just as they left it as a family of five in late April.

The house had anyway already become contaminated by then, by association. The interrogation of apartment 5A at the Mark Warner Ocean Club resort in Praia da Luz, where Madeleine vanished on the night of 3 May, had been exhaustive and unrelenting. The inner life of the architecture had been forensically examined by investigators on the ground and by being made the subject of diagrammatic illustrations, scale models, computer graphics with X-ray perspective and fly-away walls.

There had been re-enactments using actors, grainy montages on YouTube, dimly filmed guided tours of other apartments in the block with a shifty pornographic ambience ('And this *here* is the bathroom!'), the distance between apartment and tapas bar paced out by video sleuths and posted on the internet as a prompt for more superheated speculation and outlandish gossip.

The body dogs Keela and Eddie had sniffed out every inch of the interior; individual fibres had been identified and removed for investigation.

So there was that contamination of the McCanns' otherwise blameless house in the Midlands caused by the generic scene-of-crime-style overhead pictures that had been put into circulation; caused too by the transference of the atmosphere of uncanniness from the holiday flat in Praia da Luz to the house in Rothley – from one place connected with Madeleine to the other; the spectre of demonistic or magic forces.

The connection, more a mood or a suspicion up to that point, was given concrete form when, on their return to Britain, the McCanns appointed a man whose face had once been familiar to millions of viewers from the *Six O'Clock* and the *Ten O'Clock News* as their press spokesman.

Clarence Mitchell's was one of those television faces which had never registered as missing until it suddenly reappeared. For many years a thread in the broad tapestry of the national pageant, reporting mostly on the misfortunes of strangers but also the deaths of notable figures such as Jill Dando and the Queen Mother, he had eventually been reassigned to the BBC's round-the-clock, rolling news operation, *News 24*. Put on the graveyard shift newscasting through the night, one night he did the

1 a.m. and the 2 a.m. but then closed his eyes and slept through the three o'clock bulletin, after which, having served the Corporation man and boy, he had severed his ties.

Clarence – the slightly antique name was matched by a personal manner of impeccable restraint and an old-fashioned, maître-d'-like sense of deference – had first turned up in the context of the McCann story shortly before they travelled to Rome at the end of May for their St Peter's Square audience with the new Pope, Benedict XVI. He shepherded the McCanns into their place in the receiving line and in front of the cameras and fielded questions at the press conference which followed courtesy of the British Ambassador to the Holy See. For viewers, it was disconcerting to have him back on their screens as a participant in a story rather than in his accustomed role of non-aligned reporter. (This was mixed with the sense of guilt they felt at not having noticed he had gone missing in the first place.) After leaving the BBC he had taken the job of director of the Media Monitoring Unit at Number 10.

To many people Clarence Mitchell was the reporter most closely associated with the television coverage of the West murders in Gloucester in 1991. It was Mitchell who reported the developing story of the apparently respectable married couple who had been charged with murdering their daughter and burying her body under the patio in the back garden. And, after Rose West had been found guilty of murdering Heather and twelve other girls and young women (Fred West had hanged himself in prison before he could be tried), it was Clarence Mitchell who stood outside the house in Cromwell Street in Gloucester where bodies had been discovered buried in pits in the garden and under the cellar and described how the Wests had tortured and sexually abused their children over a period of many years.

So, for those with memories of this earlier Clarence Mitchell, it was strange to see him cast in the role of spokesman and media representative ('spin doctor' was a phrase that was soon used) for a couple who a few days earlier had been declared *arguidos* or official suspects by the Portuguese police investigating the disappearance of their daughter.

In his new incarnation – and Mitchell chose to demonstrate his belief in the McCanns' total innocence in a persuasive way: he resigned his government post to become their official mouthpiece soon after they returned from Portugal, his salary taken care of by a Cheshire businessman, Brian Kennedy (no relation to Kate McCann's uncle of the same name), who had made his money in doubleglazing and was now also the owner of Sale Sharks rugby club – facing the cameras with the McCanns usually now standing mutely alongside him, Clarence assumed the air of a man holding his funeral director's black silk hat considerately behind his back, a little scuffed and showing signs of wear (dandruff dusting the brim, perspiration stains dunning the pleated, satinised lining), mourning a professional future that was now well behind him, as well as the child who vanished into folklore and common fame in the family-friendly foreign resort.

The law as it stands puts no obligation on vendors to disclose a property's history. A Yorkshire couple discovered this when they attempted to sue the people who had sold them a house that had been the scene of a particularly horrific murder. Alan and Susan Sykes found out about the history of the house in Stillwell Drive, in Sandal, a suburb of Wakefield, while watching a documentary about a man who killed his adopted daughter. The programme was about Dr Samson Perera, a dental biologist at Leeds University, who murdered the little girl, Nilanthie, in 1985. The couple the Sykes had bought the house from in 2000 had decided to move two years after buying it after being filled in on its grisly past by a helpful neighbour.

Apartment 5A at the Ocean Club resort in Praia da Luz. The McCanns' family home at Orchard House in Rothley. Casa Liliana, the house belonging to the mother of Robert Murat, the first official suspect in the disappearance of Madeleine McCann in Praia, a hundred metres from the Ocean Club apartment: a dark house in a landscape of sun-soaked brilliant white render, cocooned within dense hedges and tall wire-mesh fences, bits of the hedge starting to die where people had inserted themselves into it for a better view. Myrobella, the Blairs' base for twenty-three years in the north of England, with its strategic screening and hot-wired security annexe, its air of concealment, inviting speculation. The West house in Gloucester before the council pounded it to dust, the pedestrian form of its dark shape.

Is there any way of sensing from outside, with whichever organ it might be, in which of two identical properties an atrocity has been committed? A way of telling the 'house of horror' from the 'dream home', the soap star's bolt-hole, the prime minister's residence? Does something of past events linger in the rooms, the places where they happened? Something sensed, felt, remembered, suspected, imagined, no means of perception excluded? In a room, by a wall. The uncanniness of something excluded, closed off.

After very many months, a picture of the room in the Ocean Club resort in Praia da Luz from which Madeleine had been subtracted – she had been sleeping in the bed with the twins, Sean and Amelie, sleeping either side of her in their cots at the time – was finally released. The white walls, the wall-length wardrobe, the bare floor, the wooden chair, the narrow bed, the mattress stripped, the sheets bunched, a baby-blue blanket thrown over a pregnant pillow, the little chest of drawers. What was locked and what was open? Was there an abductor? A gauze-like green curtain was it, between bed and chair, lifted on the wind, billowing in? The world's largest-ever manhunt. The town awash with rumour. The clairvoyants and the diviners. The astral seers. The texters and bloggers and the spitters of abuse.

Tony Blair announced his intention of standing down

as prime minister on 10 May, a week to the day after Madeleine's disappearance. The 3 May, the day she disappeared, was the tenth anniversary of Blair's first full day as prime minister. Overnight on 2 May 1997, he flew from his Sedgefield constituency to London; later in the day, he drove past cheering crowds to the Palace to receive the official invitation to form a government. He spent the following day, a Saturday, finalising Cabinet appointments and completing the fine-tuning of the new government.

Two big publishing events took place in the early summer of 2007. The first was the final instalment of the Harry Potter saga, *The Deathly Hallows*. (Jo Rowling's plan to have a bookmark with Madeleine's picture on it inside every copy was abandoned when it was decided that young readers would find this too distressing.) The other big bookworld push was for Alastair Campbell's 'Diaries' of his years spent spinning for Tony Blair and New Labour.

Campbell's diary entries for the summer and autumn of 1999 turned out to be dominated by the event of Cherie Blair's pregnancy and the birth the following May of Leo, the first baby born to a serving prime minister for more than a century. It becomes clear that the new baby brought Blair great solace through difficult times. But returning to Number 10 at the end of a gruelling foreign trip or a long day dealing with the foot-and-mouth crisis or strategy meetings for beginning the second Gulf War, he would sometimes return to Downing Street to find that the baby had climbed in with Cherie and he would end up picking his way through the trains and Thomas the Tank Engine toys scattered across the carpet in Leo's room and collapse exhausted into Leo's bed.

Madeleine had a plastic kitchen range in her bedroom in Rothley, a present for Christmas 2006. Leo had a plastic kitchen range in his bedroom in Downing Street, a present on his fifth birthday in 2005. Madeleine's was pink and grey. Leo's was grey and green. Madeleine had Cuddles, her pink Cuddle Cat – everything pink, her favourite colour. Leo had his cuddly ladybird toy, red with black polka-dot spots that the PM, snuggling up against it, would have to throw out of the bed.

The toy-filled room. The still warm but cooling bed. The man with executive power sleeping fitfully, alone in the narrow child's bed, twisting the sheets, spilling the blankets.

The political benefits of small wars. In the Reagan years, Dick Cheney was said to speak often, in private, on this topic. The thrusting, imprinting example of Margaret Thatcher had shown the way – standing ovations in Parliament, streets mounded with flowers thrown by ecstatic fans as the waving goddess passed. 'One of the keys to being seen as a great leader,' Dubya told his sacked biographer Mickey Herskowitz, 'is to be seen as a commander-in-chief.'

In Leo's room: the tomb chamber of an embalmed pharaonic figure, preserved in hope of resurrection. (Made in China, recalled as a potential health hazard in August 2007).

Teflon Tony. The man without a shadow. Stick with that image of Madeleine's room in the irradiated apartment block in Praia da Luz, visible even in the dark. How exposed a house looks when it becomes a taped-off scene-of-crime. How stripped of sanctity, wrote V. S. Naipaul, when a room, once intimate, becomes mere space.

The apartment is on the ground floor on a corner plot, the road running right past it.

I see what I see very clearly. But I don't know what I'm looking at.

It is a portrait of no one there.

Chapter Four

In the past he used to be able to look out of his window straight into the windows of the Follett house on the Embankment. The millionaire novelist Ken Follett, as the press invariably described him (and as he always liked to be described, as he always liked the raised foil lettering, shiny platinum and silver, the high-echelon credit card-colours on his bestselling paperbacks) lived there with his wife Barbara, the Member of Parliament for Stevenage. (She was one of 'Blair's Babes' who came in at the 1997 general election.)

In the summer there were parties, with pretty pink satin-lined marquees and softly parping riverboat-shuffle-style trad jazz bands, the chink of ice, lazily rising peals of laughter. By standing perilously close to the edge of his roof he was able to spot celebrities such as Sir Antony Sher and Salman Rushdie mingling with media folk and prominent political personalities in the gently terraced back garden.

Before she became an MP, Barbara Follett had been retained as an image consultant for Neil Kinnock and certain members of his shadow cabinet. This came to be known in the press as 'being Folletted': her decision to put the famously untelegenic shadow Trade and Industry Secretary, Robin Cook, into 'autumn tones' for his appearances in front of the media was one that came in for particular mockery.

Ken Follett, whenever he ran in to him at the newsagent's or in the post office, was always very dapper in expensive suedes and cashmere, Jermyn Street rollnecks and blazers with gold buttons and occasionally tartan slacks.

'The Folletts'. They were a diary-page staple. The buzz was with them through the Kinnock years and John Smith's brief period as leader, on into the Blair succession. But then it seems their gilded reputation started to tell against them. It didn't sit well with New Labour.

The turning point came on the night of a dinner the Blairs attended at the Folletts' handsome house on the river, soon after Tony had reached his accommodation with Gordon Brown about being the most electable face of the new hosed-down, post-ideology, voter-friendly Labour Party. The distancing of the Party from the unions over the previous ten years meant that it now had to find alternative sources of finance, and Ken Follett had been in the vanguard of fundraising from 'high value' donors. But the press had been tipped off on the night of the private dinner at his house in 1995 and the pictures of the Blairs arriving resulted in a flurry of stories about Tony and Cherie's alleged high-living in 'luvvie-land'. The pop impresario Michael Levy (later to be known as 'Lord Cashpoint') replaced Ken Follett as chief fundraiser, the Folletts were cast out of the inner circle, their garden parties became less frequent and more subdued, and towards the end of Blair's first term as prime minister the handsome house in Chelsea was sold.

Before he moved in, the new owner, an American so it was rumoured, embarked on a drastic two-year renovation. It is a prestigious property that stands on the site of Thomas Girtin's late-eighteenth-century watercolour masterpiece, *The White House at Chelsea*. Girtin died in 1802 when he was only twenty-seven. He was a friend and rival of Turner, and it was on this stretch of the river at Battersea Reach that Turner chose to spend the last six years of his life. After Turner, it was the place artists came to live.

Once or twice he had seen Francis Bacon, whose favourite model Henrietta Moraes lived around the corner, waiting by the bus stop outside the Follett house, hair oxblooded with boot-polish, carrier bag in hand. It was the same bus stop that, according to the biographies, T. S. Eliot used to use when he was a resident of Carlyle Mansions to travel to his job as poetry editor at Faber and Faber.

One afternoon, bringing the dog back from the park, he had come across Peter Sellers and his new wife Britt Ekland appraising the Follett house (although this was several years before it was known as that), craning their necks, admiring a conservatory which is built on piers and is actually part of the adjoining property, speculating (he imagined) on what it must be like to be sitting in it, drink in hand, sunk into the rattan armchairs covered in the green bamboo-pattern fabric that the then-owners had, held in suspension between misty Whistlerian river and the vast expanse of gunmetal sky, floating in a diorama of changing light. (When, after Sellers' death, Britt Ekland took up with a member of the American retro rockabilly band Stray Cats and he would sometimes spot them together looking dishevelled and hungover in the rougher pubs and cafés of the World's End – looking like vintage pictures of an off-the-rails Amy Winehouse and her drug-addled husband that ran like a flicker-frame through the whole of that summer – he would recall that other Britt who was an intimate of Princes Margaret's, one of Peter Sellers' best friends, and that other time before the Follett house was the Follett house.)

The new owner of the house gave it a startling wash of peony pink. It was the moment of Russia and China and the new super-rich Asian countries. Under the influence of globalisation, the nature of financial markets had changed. Art, for example, had become 'monetised'. Art had become an asset class comparable to stocks or real estate. Finance, he read without understanding what he was reading, was now an end it itself. It no longer needed a real economy to function because it had gone off into hyperspace, operating in a virtual world.

It was a changed, and still vertiginously changing, world. The rewards for those who knew and understood how to manipulate money were unprecedentedly massive. And Mr Studzinsky, the new owner of the handsome house at the bend of the river, was apparently a part of that world.

He had dogs. Three, and then four big dogs, giant Leonburgers which bayed and, when out for walks, loped slowly, like a pack. An elaborate system of security was installed, and a man in a uniform sent round every night to check. A trip-light was set up over the garage to interrogate every face passing in the street. Spiked fences were erected. Security cameras boxed in with metal grilles. Mature trees were swung in over the rooftops and their big rootballs buried in a line along the back of the house so that, even clinging precariously to the chimney and peering over, his view of the garden was now screened off, blocked by the new wall of trees.

The front of the house with the sweeping view of the river was in a red zone. There was no stopping. And so all exchange between outside and inside took place at the side, through the garages which were set back from the pavement, leaving a raked concrete area where the car could be washed and visiting vehicles parked. Standing by the bus stop – the same stop where Francis Bacon and, before him, T. S. Eliot (a lifelong anglophile, like Mr Studzinski) once waited – it was impossible to be unaware of the day-long comings and goings of florists and dry-cleaning people, of his driver, his butler, the first- and second-gardener, the Filipino domestics and the husband of one of them, the odd-job man, the men who walked his dogs. But never the man himself.

There were rumours. He read about him in the papers: about the Picasso collection, the Man Rays, the salons reflecting his polymath interests, 'mixing artists, authors and musicians with clergy, politicians, royalty and captains of industry . . . the Duchess of Kent and Sting; Lord Browne of BP and members of the Gucci family'. There had been a £5 million donation that summer towards the new extension at Tate Modern, of which he was a Trustee.

He heard about him from the neighbours: about the black Range Rover with the smoked windows brought up to within inches of the garage door at seven every morning; the papers fanned out just so across the back seat; the rapid acceleration. (This from a woman who lived in the Peabody buildings directly opposite who struck up a conversation with him at the newsagent's one morning. 'You have a little dog, don't you?' she said pleasantly. 'You're a writer. I see you. I'm straight opposite. You're from the same part of the world as me.') The new owner was a kind of phantom created by hearsay and rumour – a virtual owner. In this way he was entirely a creature of his time, a time that had stopped caring what companies produced; they existed now only for buying and selling. Hedge funds. Fungible assets. Private equity. The derivatives market. Mr Studzinski was said to be a master of modern financial engineering; a genius at the new prime minister Gordon Brown's pet subject, fiscal arithmetic.

These were the reasons the directors of Northern Rock retained Studzinki's services as an adviser when there was a run on the bank in the middle of September, with savers camping overnight outside branches all across the country to withdraw their money. It was the first run on a British bank in more than a century, a scandal of mismanagement that was the result (it seemed, although it was initially difficult to work out how) of something called 'subprime mortgages' in America. Divorced from the jargon, this turned out to be the practice of lending money to low-income homeowners, many of them black, who could never afford to pay it back.

The Bank of England had to pump £26 billion of tax-payers' money into Northern Rock to keep it afloat. Studzinski, by then head of investment banking at Blackstone, the private equity group, was among those who had to weigh up the claims of the various groups and conglomerates bidding to buy the bank. Whatever the eventual outcome, Studzinski himself couldn't lose. The advisers to the consortium led by Sir Richard Branson were known to be getting a minimum £5 million even if the deal fell through. Studzinski's guarantee was understood to be at the very least double that.

After his obsession with secrecy and his wealth, the other best-known thing about Studzinski was the depth of his religious faith. He devoted time to prayer and meditation in the morning and again at night. He was a devout Catholic who had had a private chapel built in his house. Pride of place in the chapel was given to two candlesticks which had once belonged to the founder of the Jesuits, Ignatius Loyola. He was made a Knight of the Order of St Gregory for a record of good works, including thirty years working with the homeless, and the Catholic church in Britain was said to be so beholden to him that Cardinal Cormac Murphy-O'Connor, the Church's leader in England and Wales, would change his diary to fit in with John Studzinski's.

At the beginning of the summer, the house abutting Mr Studzinski's – the house with the floating conservatory that from the outside looks as if it belongs to him – was sold and a team of builders moved in. The builders were mainly Polish and at lunchtimes and cigarette breaks they would gather as a group at the front of the house. He grew used to seeing them, lounging round chatting and smoking, gathered around a radio playing Polish music. It was something new in the street, new music, the smells of different foods and cigarettes, but a scene familiar in every part of London, where house prices in some areas – this area was one of them – had been increasing by as much as 30 per cent a year.

When the work on the house was nearing completion – the appearance of two women among the workforce suggested they had reached the stage of making good and skimming, and the house was close to being liveable in again – he bumped into a neighbour from his block who told him that earlier that evening (it was a Sunday, her first back from Bernard Arnault's yacht on the Côte d'Azure) he had spotted Cherie Blair and another woman coming out of the house adjoining Studzinski's.

Were the Blairs considering a move to Chelsea, into the house next door to what had once been known as the

Follett house, the house that they had had to stop visiting twelve years earlier because it placed them too close to what the papers called 'luvvie-land'? There had been reports of them being shown over a country pile called Winslow Hall in Berkshire and of Tony becoming 'the local country squire'. (The former Conservative leader Ian Duncan Smith had performed the opening ceremony at the local pub, the Betsey Wynne; his wife is called Betsy). Tony had apparently recently been spotted looking for a possible headquarters for his Blair Foundation to promote 'inter-faith dialogue' in Manchester Square, where he inspected the former Spanish Embassy at number 23.

But money was thought to be an issue. Cherie had interrupted the family holiday at Sir Cliff's Barbados villa in the early part of the summer to fly to the US to give three speeches. In the early autumn it would be announced that she had agreed a rumoured £1 million deal to write her memoirs. A month later Tony would at last announce that he had signed up to write his. The contract was brokered by a Washington lawyer called Robert Barnett who had secured the $12 million deal for Bill Clinton's *My Life*. Among Barnett's other clients were Barack Obama, Alan Greenspan and Benazir Bhutto. Blair's contract was thought to be worth around £5 million. The publisher was Random House; its UK wing is headed by Gail Rebuck, who is married to Tony's close ally and former pollster Lord Gould.

But in early September, according to some of the papers, Cherie was still 'tearing her hair out' over her husband's decision to resurrect his battered reputation by attempting to negotiate peace in the Middle East 'rather than make the millions she craves'. His envoy role was backed up with a substantial budget drawn from a UN-administered trust fund: his fourteen-strong multinational team were in the process of taking over the entire fourth floor of East Jerusalem's lovely old American Colony Hotel; an exercise treadmill had been installed, and ornate and gilded Ottoman-looking sofas; there was a shaded terrace screened with newly planted olive and fig saplings. But his peacemaker role was unsalaried. The various foundations carrying his name were going to distribute money, not bring it in. The registered domain name blairfoundation.org remained unused.

Cherie's 'go-getting American manager', Martha Greene, was said to be considering offers for her to appear in adverts to endorse products, Fergie-style, in the States. With close to £5 million of mortgages on the properties they already owned, and work on their post-Downing Street home in Connaught Square still incomplete, it seemed unlikely that a move to Chelsea was on the cards.

Far more likely was that Mr Studzinski, a prominent Catholic like Cherie herself, a man with an excess of money – a man with the magic of always being able to make more money, of the type of whom the Blairs had always been in awe – had annexed the house next door to his own with the idea of the former prime minister using it as the headquarters of one of his charities. (Myrobella, the Blairs' house in Trimdon – opened up to the light, security barriers removed, police gatehouse demolished – was slated to become the home of his sports foundation for local young people, run by Blair's constituency agent, John Burton, a retired PE teacher.)

In early June, shortly after the McCanns had their photo of Madeleine blessed by the Pope at a public audience in St Peter's Square, Tony Blair had had a private audience with Benedict XVI as part of his 'European farewell tour'. It was rumoured then that he had been received into the Church during his visit to the Vatican. That wasn't true. But by September and Cherie's viewing of the house on Cheyne Walk, Blair was taking instruction – 'formal doctrinal and spiritual preparation for his reception into full communion' is how it would be described in the official confirmation of his conversion to Catholicism, when it came just before Christmas – from Msgr Mark O'Toole, private secretary to Cardinal Cormac Murphy-O'Connor.

Boris is a dachshund whose belly is about two inches off the floor. He's a miniature rough-haired. He often stops to chat to Boris's owner while both their dogs take it in turns to mark the gatepost of the Studzinki house. This usually happens around midnight, about the time the night buses are starting to run.

Boris is owned by a short, stout young woman with a distracted, eccentric Hattie Jacques sort of personality; scattiness with hints of depth. She hadn't said she was an actress (he hadn't said he was a writer) and so he didn't know what she did until, after he had already known her for two years, he turned on the television and was sure he had spotted her buried in the body of somebody who looked very like Ann Widdecombe and nothing like herself.

The programme was *The Thick of It*, a satire on the Blair government ('a foul-mouthed piss-take of Britain's politics of panic', in the words of one reviewer), and she was playing one of the central figures, some sort of flak-catcher or spin-doctor, disguised by a blonde wig and a nubby business suit and without the glasses she normally wore.

The setting for the series is the fictitious Department of Social Affairs and Citizenship (DoSAC). The main characters are a pathologically aggressive and domineering Number 10 enforcer, obviously based on Alastair Campbell; and 'Hugh Abbott', a blundering minister heading the department, who is continually trying to do his job under the jaundiced eye of the abusive spin-doctor-in-chief. But by the time he caught up with the programme, the minister had been written out because the actor playing him, Chris Langham, was due to be tried on charges of indecent assault and downloading indecent images of children. At his trial in August the jury were told that the video clips, which ranged in length from three seconds to six minutes, included the torture and rape of a teenage girl, the sexual abuse of a seven-year-old and an assault on a bound-and-gagged child of about twelve.

Langham was represented by the 'celebrity lawyer' Angus McBride of Kingsley Napley and in September was sentenced to ten months in prison (reduced to six on appeal). Less than a fortnight later, McBride and his partner in the firm, Michael Caplan, QC, were being retained by Kate and Gerry McCann who had said they were committed to raising public awareness of child torture and abuse and the international trafficking of children.

While working, successfully, to prevent General Pinochet's extradition to Spain to face torture charges, Michael Caplan's only comment on defending a man accused of such acts was: 'I have a duty to a client, just as a surgeon does to a patient'.

Mr Studzinki's rock-star guests don't have to travel far to his networking salons at his house. Both Bryan Ferry and Eric Clapton live only a street away, close neighbours of Kate Middleton.

Bryan Adams lives in a fag-ash and sticky-carpet pub he used to use, modernised and minimalised now, presenting a blank face to the world, fifty yards further along the Embankment. In the early days, the seventy million who clicked onto findmadeleine.com in the first month saw the Madeleine eye logo, the defect in the right eye incorporated into the two O's of 'Look' in the slogan 'Looking for Madeleine' and heard Bryan Adams singing 'Look into my eyes/ You will see what you mean to me . . .', the first lines of his multi-platinum, chart-topping single '(Everything I Do) I Do It for You'. They had asked and he had agreed that the McCanns could use it as the soundtrack to the official website dedicated to collecting donations from the public and to bringing home the little girl.

The start of the summer saw a new rock-star arrival – or, rather, the return of one who had done more than most to establish Chelsea's raffish reputation in the Sixties. Mick Jagger had been living with Marianne Faithfull in a house on Cheyne Walk when he was arrested with Keith Richard and the art dealer Robert Fraser and tried for possessing heroin (in Fraser's case) and marijuana. Now, forty years later, he was back, as Mr Studzinski's next-door-neighbour-but-one, and he immediately ruffled feathers with a planning application to cut down a long-established set of magnolia trees in the back garden of the £10 million property he was about to begin renovating. The idea was to house a swimming pool in a building resembling a Georgian orangery, its roof supported by neoclassical pillars decorated with Roman-style engravings, and the trees would have to go.

He learned all this when the buzzer went one afternoon and it was a photographer from a national paper wanting access to the roof. He wanted to get onto the roof to train a lens on Jagger's back garden, zoom in on the offending trees, fire off a few shots. Millionaire rock giant versus the little people. Kind of thing.

'Studz' has a chapel for the sake of his spiritual well-being. He craned in a stand of trees. Jagger wants a pool to stay in shape. He wants to fell the magnolias. Their pastoral welfare.

Mr Studzinski has a private chapel for daily prayer and meditation, a refuge from the day-to-day of cutting deals.

He has a hotline to Cardinal Cormac Murphy-O'Connor, the leader of Catholics in England and Wales. He has found solace in his Catholic faith.

In the immediate aftermath of Madeleine's disappearance, Kate and Gerry found sanctuary in the pretty little Nossa Senhora da Luz church at the edge of the sea. The priest gave them a key to the church to allow them to be able to go there at any time of the night or day and be alone with their thoughts. They felt cosseted, Gerry said. It was about challenging the negatives, banishing the blackest and darkest thoughts. They were surrounded by the Ambassador, the consul, PR, crisis management, journalists, the police. The church was a refuge; a place to get away, to be with Madeleine again, to escape. The priest kept a flickering image of Madeleine thrown from a projector onto a wall, a beautiful gesture. Late at night, and in the middle of the night, when they sometimes went, waves crashed on the beach. Cardinal Cormac Murphy-O'Connor's Westminster office arranged for them to travel to see the Pope.

Kate said: 'I wish I could roll back time and go back to the day before Madeleine was abducted. I would slow down time. I would get a really good look around and have a really good think. And I'd think: Where are you? Who are you? Who is secretly watching my family? Because someone was watching my family very, very carefully. And taking notes.'

The collective memory of any recent generation, wrote

Howard Singerman, has now become the individual memory of each of its members, for the things that carry the memory are marked not by the privacy, the specificity and insignificance of Proust's madeleine, but precisely by their publicness and their claim to significance.

The generalised sense of loss that pervaded the summer.

'Praia' meaning 'beach'. 'Luz' meaning 'light'.

Wishing it all undone, healed again.

Chapter Five

Gordon and Tony. Tony and Peter. Gordon and Charlie. Ally and Tony. Peter and Gordon. Charlie and Ed. The PM and David B. Gordon and Ed. Ed hates Tony. Tony complains that his treatment by Ed with Gordon's smirking connivance is like being an abused and bullied wife.

When the Kennedy court historian Arthur M. Schlesinger's *Diaries* were published in the United States in the summer, eyebrows were raised at a quote from Henry Kissinger about Richard Nixon: 'He was unquestionably a weird president, but he was not a weak president. But everything was weird in that slightly homosexual, embattled atmosphere of the White House.'

What could Kissinger have been driving at, commentators wondered? What did he mean?

The millions of devoted fans of *Little Britain* already had a clue. One of the most popular of the cast of regular characters in the BBC comedy was Sebastian, a predatory, protective, queeny gay aide to a good-looking young prime minister who bore a strong resemblance to Tony Blair.

Peter Mandelson was the only 'out' homosexual at the heart of the New Labour project. ('I know he's . . . that way,' Neil Kinnock said to Roy Hattersley at the conclusion of the 1985 interview that saw Mandelson appointed as Labour's director of communications, 'but why does he have to flaunt it?') But there was an unmistakeable homoerotic inflection to many of the key relationships which defined the Blair governments.

A number of critics identified this as one of the most surprising revelations to emerge from Alastair Campbell's 'Diaries'. 'It's not a gay thing exactly, but it's not the opposite of a gay thing,' John Lanchester wrote in August in his review of the The Blair Years in the London Review of Books. The book was 'full of dark-haired men shouting at each other . . . bursting into tears, having make-up heart-to-hearts, saying bitchy things about each other behind each other's backs . . . The cover picture is part of this, [Blair] looking up at [Campbell] with an expression of submissive yearning that verges on the pornographic.'

Another reviewer wrote teasingly about what she interpreted as Campbell's 'crush' on Bill Clinton. 'If Brokeback Mountain was set in Westminster and starred Rock Hudson and Judy Garland,' wrote Nirpal Dhaliwal of the The Blair Years in the London Evening Standard, 'it still wouldn't be gayer than this.'

It had long been a convention among political correspondents to describe the heterosexual bond between Gordon Brown and Tony Blair as a 'marriage'. 'The intimate story of a political marriage' was the subtitle of James

Naughtie's book *The Rivals*. The section headings of the crucial chapter devoted to Gordon Brown in Anthony Seldon's biography of Blair are titled, with a nod towards the true-romance magazines, 'Perfect Union', 'Seven-Year Itch', 'Living Apart', 'Marriage of Convenience', 'Love's Labour's Lost', and so on.

The relationship between the two men had to be described as a marriage, wrote Naughtie, because there was 'no other way of explaining the deep mystery of how their moments of political intimacy are often disturbed by tensions and arguments that seem to well up from a history in the partnership that only the two of them can feel fully or understand'. Seldon chronicles 'the exceptional regard they had for each other', how they were variously described as 'joined at the hip' or 'the brothers'. He writes about 'the joy, laughter and indeed love in their relationship' between 1983, when they both entered Parliament as young MPs, and 1990, when the balance within the relationship began to shift in Blair's favour.

It became a commonplace during his decade as prime minister for people to remark on Blair's acting skills and marvel at his ability to emerge from political and personal meltdowns weirdly unscathed. He appeared charming, relaxed, well-mannered, always smiling; he seemed gifted with an innate sense of knowing that it's not what's *there* that counts, it's what's projected. (What his mentor, Mandelson, famously referred to as 'creating the truth' and the former Labour chancellor Denis Healey publicly called 'merde de boeuf – bullshit, bullshit and nothing else'.) His chancellor, on the other hand – 'a nail-biting, badly-dressed hermit', as somebody once described him, 'with the social skills of a whelk' – had presentational difficulties.

'He looks like somebody hung him in a cupboard overnight and he jumps out in the morning with his suit all bunched up and starts running around saying, "I want to be prime minister".' After celebrity-PM Tony, with the permatan and the TV smile, it had come to Brown to be the embodiment of piety, careerism and a darkling soul.

But the gods seemed to be with him when he took over from Blair at the end of June. The crises that piled up around Gordon Brown in his first weeks in office – the attempted terrorist attacks on London and Glagow, the summer floods in the midlands and the north, foot-and-mouth: fire, flood and pestilence, a marvellous start for a son of the manse, as a number of people pointed out – these gifts from the gods required him to be thunder-faced, decisive, dogged, statesmanlike. The one thing they didn't require him to do was the thing he had always had a problem with: they didn't require him to smile.

Watching Brown struggling to uncloud his counte-nance with a sunny smile – his former Cabinet colleague Robin Cook once described him as having a 'face like a wet winter's morning in Fife' – became the recurring bad sight of the year; a car-crash moment waiting to happen at each and every photo-op.

A couple of months into his premiership, Brown and Ed Balls, his close political ally and newly appointed, still learning-on-the-job Children's Minister, visited a factory where neets and youths on asbos were being shown how to dismember a chicken. The camera pulled round behind the white-coated figure doing the dismembering, panned from the tallow yellow skin of the chicken along the butcher's hairy arm to the faces of the bored and bolshy apprentices, before pulling slowly back to reveal the prime minister and his faithful Cabinet colleague grinning their grins of commitment, confidence and compassion. The report contained flash photography. Brown's grin was fixed, as always, as a grimace; there was some gurning, a movement that suggested chewing, the clearing of a shred of tomato skin maybe from in front of his bottom teeth; a hint that if anything upset his rather delicately balanced equilibrium he could at any second and without warning revert to being Bad Gordon – the Gordon of kicking the furniture and control-freak tendencies; meanspirited, domineering; the Gordon of the shaking hand, the clouded mien, prone to sudden and terrible rages.

It was a terrible summer and a peculiar time. It was a time that found its symbol in the prime minister's anxiety-shrouded, tortured, tombstone grin. It hurt to smile. He lost the sight of his left eye as the result of a school rugby accident: a bang on the head caused both retinas to become detached and one of the four operations he underwent meant that a smile no longer triggered the appropriate facial muscles. It pained him to smile. It was hard. It was painful to watch. But it was necessary if he was going to dispel his stubborn image of being grumpy, cold and aloof (and stubborn). An analogue politician in a digital age. Old Gordon. The cracked countenance was meant to betoken a transformation. No longer damaged in some unspecified way; no longer 'psychologically flawed' as his many enemies, taking their lead from Alastair Campbell, had long spun against him. 'Not flash, just Gordon.'

The task was to rebrand him as a politician. To reposition him in the market. To re-enchant the commodity by tapping into the same hankering for a grainy tangibility to the artefact that had seen the fetishisation of other antiquated analogue formats like vinyl and tape cassettes. Upfront depth in a world of fake surfaces. Urgent seriousness in frivolous times. The analogue and artisanal, wrote Simon Reynolds, are equated with a sort of spiritual integrity. Back to the future. Turning his pathologies into assets, his deficits into advantages. That had been the plan.

The smile was meant to be reassuring. He was a man with a reputation for reading spreadsheets, surveys of the immediate and long-term trends in small corporate manufacturing, IMF reports, for relaxation. Favourite author, Alan Greenspan, former head of the Federal Reserve Board: 'I have always argued that an up-to-date set of the most detailed estimates for the latest available quarter is far more useful for forecasting accuracy than a more sophisticated model structure.' Words to live by.

He needed to be warmed up. To smile is to be human. A sense of humour – he really needed to get one of those. The Gordon grin. It was supposed to offer warmth and reassurance. But it repeatedly misfired. Not once, or some-times, but all the time. 'Liberty is the first and founding value of our country. Security is the first duty of our government.' Paint-stripper grin. 'A system of this kind seems to have the potential to close the aching gap between the potential benefits of transplant surgery in the UK and the limits imposed by our current system of consent.' Stony gargoyle smile.

The separation between what he was saying and what his face was doing added up to a disturbing disjunction. The result was sinister. Pathological. It was something new and unwanted loosed to roam unchecked in the culture. Gerry started to think when he made his 9 p.m. check on the twins and Madeleine, her abductor must have already been in the room, lurking in the shadows behind the bed-room door, waiting, watching. A new sense of apprehension and unsettlement seeping through into everyday life. A smile like the brass plate on a coffin. *Wheeeere is he? I love Tony Bair! . . . No, I don't like Gordon Brown!*

Norman Mailer remembered Richard Nixon as 'a church usher, of the variety who would twist a boy's ear after removing him from church'. And as the months ticked past – the Brown bounce in the polls crashing by November into a 14-point deficit; the honeymoon souring, the smile hung on the damaged face muscles growing ever more berserk, ever more pleading; hair colour warmed up and toned down, hair newly volumised and shingled – Nixon is the politician Brown came to increasingly resemble.

Nixon was the first politician of the television age to consciously recognise that political success had come to depend almost entirely on the presentation of a pleasing personality. The issues merely provide the occasions for testing the personal appeal of the contenders: everything hinges on the tremble of the hand or voice, the slick of sweat on brow or upper lip, the general air of ease or unease under performance pressure. ('Body language'. That was what all the commentators said they would be looking out for at Gordon's Camp David meeting with George Bush in July. Gordon's graphic body language, its stammer and stutter). The presentation of a pleasing personality thing was not news that Nixon revelled in, noted Richard Schickel, because he had enough self-awareness to recognise that a pleasing personality was precisely what he did not possess.

Nixon's problem was himself. Not what he said but the man he was. The camera portrayed him clearly. It showed a man who craved regulation, who flourished best in the darkness, behind clichés, behind phalanxes of young advisers. But to his amazement, Nixon discovered that a candidate no longer needed a personality of his own in order to stand for public office. There were people now who could make one up for you.

Nixon survived, despite his flaws, wrote Joe McGinnis in his account of the 1968 US presidential election, because he was tough and smart, and – some said – dirty when he had to be. Also because there was nothing else he knew. A man to whom politics is all there is in life will almost always beat one to whom it is only an occupation.

It wasn't a new Gordon Brown that was at the top of the polls halfway though his first hundred days. It was the old Gordon with his strengths looking stronger and his negatives blurred by the firm, mature, no-nonsense way he had reacted to the car-bomb scares and the floods.

Then, early in August, the third major crisis piled in: pestilence. An outbreak of foot-and-mouth disease was confirmed at a cattle farm in Surrey and a national ban immediately imposed on the movement of all livestock. It happened on the first day of Brown's bucket-and-spade holiday with his wife Sarah and their young sons John and Fraser in Dorset. There had just been time for a photo opportunity on the beach at Weymouth (the PM in dark suit and polished black leather Oxfords: he only has two outfits in his wardrobe – one is a suit, the other is a suit without a tie; not wearing a tie is as informal as he gets) when he had to rush away to listen in to a meeting of Cobra, the government's civil emergency committee. The following morning he again had to deny himself a day at the beach buying 99s and building sandcastles and travelled instead to London to chair a full Cobra meeting. He was not seen on Chesil beach the next day, or the day after. The buckets and spades were packed and the holiday abandoned.

It would later emerge that he had slipped away, back to Scotland, and was spending August, the deadest month in politics, bunkered in his constituency office in Cowdenbeath High Street, close to Kirkcaldy where he grew up.

Kirkcaldy was once famous for the smells of the linoleum factory which was one of the chief employers in the town. Cowdenbeath used to be dominated by a pit, whose extensive workings were adjacent to Central Park, the football ground. The area is now landscaped, beautified, and almost completely open. Cowdenbeath is hardly more than a village, in which Central Park seems disproportionately large and looming and, ominously, since the death of the coalmine, quieter, cleaner, more alone.

The rumpled suit, the dusty box files, the calcified kettle, the tottering piles of yellowing papers. The stones marking the entrance to the old pit, which was finally exhausted in 1960; the shop-front office, the silent stadium, his minders yawning, kicking their heels.

It resurrected images of Old Gordon, the bedsit swot, got a briefcase for Christmas and loved it, forty-two years old the day he was born. The Gordon who often seemed to bristle with displeasure when surrounded by human beings rather than Treasury reports and breakdowns of costings, given to brooding, introspection and suspicion. He'd always have his homework done and he'd never let you copy.

Gordon by then, however, had made a marvellous new friend who would protect him in the playground and had provided him with an ingenious solution to what until then had appeared an intractable image problem. The attempt to ram a car bomb into the arrivals hall at Glasgow airport had thrown up SuperSmeato, an instant, home-grown hero. And SuperSmeato – working-class,

Scottish, plain-talking man of the people ('This is Glasgow! We'll just set aboot ye!') had quickly been drafted in as Gordon's secret weapon: his cursing, sweating, horny-handed sharer-self.

'Now John has a message for any would-be terrorist', says the interviewer in a voice-over. And John says: 'You come to Glasgow . . . Glasgow doesn't accept this, d'you know what I mean? This is Glasgow you know . . . so we'll set about you. You know? That's it.'

'Nothing, like something,' Philip Larkin wrote, 'happens anywhere.' John Smeaton lives with Mum, Catherine, and Dad, Iain, on a pleasant, nothing estate in Erskine on the outskirts of Glagow. He had a going-nowhere job as a baggage handler at Glasgow airport, overseeing the loading and offloading of thousands of bags a day. It was a job he had been coasting along in for twelve years. He was now thirty-one. So since he was nineteen he had been in the same routine of getting up, going to work, grafting inside the aircraft, clearing the bags out, grabbing a sly smoke and then waiting for the next load to put in, at the beginning forever cracking his head or his back. At school he was a dreamer and had failed to apply himself. He left school at sixteen and started an apprenticeship as a joiner. He left at nineteen with a belief that he was being exploited and was taken on as 'hold fodder' at the airport.

The day he became the Smeatonator started as a day like any other. It was a Saturday, Gordon Brown's first in office. On 30 June Gordon Brown had been prime minister for seventy-two hours. In the early hours of Friday a green Mercedes primed with petrol and nails and cans of propane gas had been parked outside the Tiger Tiger nightclub in central London. A second car, similarly primed, had been discovered in a side-street, just around the corner. On the Saturday, just after three, the flaming Jeep Cherokee had been aimed at the main terminal building at Glasgow airport.

Smeato had done something unusual for him: he had screwed up. Saturday is always a busy day, but this one was even busier. It was the first day of the school holiday in Scotland. The arrivals hall was mobbed, his gang were working flat-out and, because he was working so hard (all those golfers, all those sets of clubs, forty or fifty sets to deal with on some flights) he managed to misread one of the screens showing departure times. Either the flight is going to have to be delayed or the golfers' plane is going to have to leave without their clubs. He feels such a jessie. It's a no-brainer job but he takes pride in doing it. He feels so peed out. So he has a cigarette. He goes outside and has a wee ciggie. When that's finished he flames up another one. And that's when, after two or three draws, this fucking fuckbag of a terrorist cunt – something Allah, something Allah – these bastards, doctors mind, turn their car into the terminal building which is packed with families off for their summer holiday.

There is a sort of screeching, a lot of commotion, a big bang. He looks around to his left and sees a four-by-four that's on fire. As he runs to help, he sees one of the men in the car get out and hit a policeman – he's been a lot of years at the airport, these policemen are his friends, and besides which you can't stand back anyways and see the law fall: the law falls, we all fall – he sees a man of Arab appearance egress the vehicle and start whackin this polis in the face. And so what are you going to do, he's going to get the boot in – he wears the steel toe-caps to work – and some other guy banjoes him, banjaxes the cunt nae bother. Then he sees another man, on fire on the other side of the Jeep, bits of his flesh peeling away, blackened flesh, the smell of burning, the intensity of the heat, a taxi driver hosing him down. A man turning to charcoal. A human ember. But still throwing punches, his skin on fire and still fighting, very, very determined. You're nae hitting the polis mate, there's nae chance . . . Boof! Take that home to Allah. You have a duty to care. That's what you're told in the airport.

Of course it fucking all went fucking off then, the T-shirts and the websites, the world and its granny wanting him to give them high-fives, the folks going through Paypal to stand him thousands of pints at the airport Holiday Inn which he passed on to the lads at Erskine hospital back from Iraq with fucked-up heads and broken bodies and shattered families, the real heroes.

For a while right after 9/11, New York City firemen attained authentic hero status: the generic 'FDNY' secured a position analogous to the one individual heroes used to occupy. But then there was the marketing of 'Calendar of Heroes' showing real firemen decked out in their gear but stripped to the waist and invitingly posed for their admirers. Real heroes today, wrote Thomas de Zengotita, must become stars if they are to exist in public culture at all. That is, they must perform. But as soon as they do that, they can't compete with the real stars – who *are* performers.

In July Smeato appeared at the Edinburgh fringe as himself in a comedy chat-show. Many in the audience wore their slogan T-shirts – 'We'll Set Aboot Yi', 'Proudly Banjoing Terrorists Since 2007' – which they got him to sign afterwards in the bar.

A week or two later Gerry McCann flew in to make what was described as a 'very uncomfortable' appearance at the Edinburgh Television Festival, using a media jolly-up to appeal to the media he had used to keep Madeleine's face in the papers to back off and leave his family alone. It was becoming the 'Kate and Gerry Show', he told a mesmerised audience, and that wasn't going to bring Madeleine home. ('Madeleine': what was it about the way he said this word, the Glaswegian intonation, the pugnacious three syllables – Muh-duh-luhn – so far from the softer, feminised French pronunciation, staunin' up for himsel', the 'Wha daur meddle wi' me' jutting jaw? Gerry the hard man, Smeato the hard man hero.) He was wearing the yellow Madeleine ribbon pinned on his jacket, along with the green ribbon which was the Portuguese symbol of hope; he had the yellow Madeleine wristband on his wrist. (People would still want the Madeleine bands even if she was found, policeman's son Calum MacRae, eighteen, responsible for the campaign's website and distribution network for Madeleine merchandise, will tell the local press. Her face is a mark. It's everywhere.)

The first call from Downing Street came at the beginning of August. On 2 August Smeats had been booked to appear on *Richard and Judy* and, because it was his first time, he brought to the sofa a scalding flush and perspiration that boiled the make-up clean off: perspiration streamed down his face, his eyes screwed against it and the strong light.

From the studios he was driven straight to Number 10. After a brief wait the prime minister himself appeared, urged him to call him 'Gordon' and showed him into his favourite Thatcher Study, where it was just the two of them alone with the dying light and the most traditional of posh paintings, all dating from the seventeenth to early nineteenth centuries and selected by the prime minister personally from the Government Art Collection: the *Portrait of Edward Montagu, First Earl of Sandwich* has pride of place above the mantelpiece; above the door is Thomas Hofland's *Warwick Castle*, on the right are John Wooton's *Italianate Landscape* and, below this, John Laporte's *Welsh Scene, Pont Aberglaslyn*.

Richard Branson got in touch and kindly offered Smeato a first-class seat to New York when he was invited to attend the sixth anniversary ceremony of 9/11. At the end of the month, Number 10 were in touch again, extending an invitation to the party conference in Bournemouth, although he was to keep this to himself and tell nobody where he was going. This was to allow Gordon Brown the *coup de théâtre* of 'unveiling' him a few minutes into his keynote speech at conference, his first as prime minister. 'When the terrorists tried to attack Scotland's biggest airport, they were answered by the courage of the police and the firefighters – and a baggage handler named John Smeaton.' Rapturous applause. 'That man, that hero John Smeaton is here with us today – and on behalf of our country, John, I want to thank you.'

The standing ovation was led by Sarah, the prime minister's wife, who had been seated beside him. And a month later Sarah Brown was one of the judges, along with Fiona Phillips of GMTV, of the *Daily Mirror*'s 'Pride of Britain' Awards which recognised Smeato's bravery with a statuette. Smeato in the kilt and sporran, Carol Vorderman making the inevitable crack about his legs ('Get a loada those legs, girls!'). The Browns were there in person to present the award to him, and the following morning he joined his fellow heroes on another visit to Number 10. 'I'll be able to show them round,' he joked, although the pictures would show him looking hot and embarrassed and blushing to the roots of his red-tinged hair.

On his first visit the prime minister had asked him whether he had been born in Glasgow and, when he said he had, he told him that he had been born in Glasgow too. The Smeatons lived in Bishopton, near a farm. In the summer it was two-man tag in the woods and in winter it was snowball fights between the neighbouring roads. You didn't play on computer games, you played outside. Now most kids are just into *The X Factor* and 'let's be famous'. But he'd had a wee touch of what's it's like to be famous, and it's not particularly great.

'I think we're moving from this period when celebrity matters, when people have become famous for being famous,' Gordon Brown said in an interview a few weeks before he became prime minister. 'I think you can see that in other countries, too, people are moving away from that to what lies behind the character and the personality. It is a remarkable culture where people appear on television and are famous simply for the act of appearing on television.'

By his second visit to Number 10 in October, SuperSmeato was wishing he could just stay at home and play on his Xbox for a week. Have a few nights in his own bed. Even better, he would be up in the north of Scotland, fly-fishing. His mobile would be back at home, switched off, and nobody would know where he was. 'At first you want to hide,' he said, 'but as the applause grows, you realise that you've got to take it in good grace. It would be rude to complain, wouldn't it?'

John ('That man, that hero') and Gordon ('What a guy'). Gordo and Smeato. The only real touch he had on things. One of the few. They were coming from the same place.

A month after taking over from Tony Blair, Gordon Brown flew to Washington for two days of meetings at Camp David with President Bush. It was his first trip abroad as prime minister, and there was high anticipation to see how Gordon-and-George would play as a follow-up to the long-running but universally panned, increasingly reviled, George-and-Tony show.

In the run-up to the trip, hardly anybody, in print or on television, failed to mention Blair's own first visit to Camp David after Bush had been elected in 2000, or to re-run footage of it. Tony had decided to dress casual for the occasion and had turned out in too-tight blue Wrangler cords ('bollock-crushing' was a description used at the time) which he attempted to wear with an insouciant, bandy-legged cow-poke swagger. Bush meanwhile wore the presidential brown leather bomber jacket and shit-kicker Texan snakeskin boots. The 'Village People' sniggers became front-page headlines the following day when, responding to a question about what he believed the two men had in common, Bush memorably replied: 'Well, we both use Colgate toothpaste.'

'People are going to be wondering how you know that, George,' Blair piped up flirtatiously just-like-that after the hilarity subsided. Memories of this earlier encounter seemed strangely to colour the coverage of Bush–Brown – GB–GB – six years later.

Gordon, it was generally recognised, didn't 'do' casual or small talk. He was an Americanist but other than that he usually didn't 'do' abroad. As Chancellor, he never stayed at embassies anywhere. Even on his visits to Washington on World Bank and other business, he shunned the opulence of the British Ambassador's residence on Massachusetts Avenue in favour of a hotel.

Bush's people had responded to the problem by inviting him to a 'sleep-over' at the presidential retreat in Maryland with dinner *à deux* in the Laurel Cabin with the president on the Sunday night.

Prior to to the trip, Foreign Office minister Mark Malloch-Brown (one of several non-Labour figures Gordon Brown had brought into his 'big tent' to counter his control-freak reputation) had warned that London would no longer be 'joined at the hip' to the Bush White House. To signal this, at Brown's request, prime minister and president were to wear suits and address each other formally. This was intended to reinforce the message that the relationship from now on would be strictly business; that Brown did not want to be Bush's buddy and that the 'special relationship' would be between Britain and the US rather than between Number 10 and the White House. Turning pathologies into assets. So what would happen? In the absence of any personal chemistry, the answer, it seemed to be unanimously agreed, would lie in the body language of the two men.

'Gordon and George spend their first night together' was the *Observer*'s headline on the Sunday of Brown's departure for Washington. 'Today Gordon Brown arrives in America for his first sleep-over with a new leader,' Andrew Rawnsley's column friskily began. 'They have had a brief encounter behind closed doors at the White House before Mr Brown became prime minister . . . but this will be the first time – metaphorically and literally – that Gordon and George have spent the night together.'

The tone of larky innuendo, looking back nostalgically perhaps to both the Clinton frolics and the days when George and Tony obliged with such lively copy, was kept up by the BBC's political editor, Nick Robinson, who, in his commentary of the touch-down in Washington, remarked that 'Gordon Brown was accompanied not by his wife, but by a young man – the new Foreign Secretary, as it happens.'

Even the weatherman got in on the act. When the Camp David press conference the following day was delayed for unknown reasons and BBC *News 24* cut away to the weather, the forecaster opened with: 'Maybe they've had a tiff.'

When they finally did appear, it was striding across an expanse of lawn, past the presidential helicopter and saluting marines, exuding manly purpose and mutual bonhomie. It was his backyard, and the president immediately assumed control. He announced that he had found the prime minister to be not at all 'dour and awkward' as reported: 'He's a humorous Scotsman.'

Mr Bush slumped hand-in-chin against his lectern, looking like Dean Martin propping up the bar in an all-night joint, one foot hooked over the other. Mr Brown stood as erect as Andy Stewart singing one of his bracing Scottish skirls, buttoned-down, whey-faced, reading from prepared notes printed in the extra-large type he depends on because of his reduced sight; at one point a breeze licked them and they started to blow away; acting to catch them was the only unrehearsed gesture the prime minister allowed himself. He was the model of propriety and solemn authority. He would leave pleased with his performance, and relieved. But Bush had an amused glint in his eye throughout. And, sure enough, there was a small time-bomb, innocent in itself but suggestive of all Gordon's once and future vulnerabilities, quietly ticking away.

The flight home on the chartered BA 767 was jolly. The PM and his party sat up-front in the first-class cabin. The press, as usual, were assigned to the other side of the curtain, in steerage. They had filed; the working part of the trip was over; drink was taken.

An empty seat in economy was occupied by a large box wrapped in gold paper. About halfway into the trip a few of the press contingent started to speculate what could be in it. They weighed it, gave it exploratory pokes and got others started on guessing what it could be. The drinks kept coming from the galley. Finally, after a great deal of persuading, in mid-Atlantic they got a young female member of the Number 10 press office to let them take a look. She loosened the paper and lifted the lid. A *Mail* photographer snatched a shot. The laughter from the reptiles' cabin could be heard all the way home.

As a souvenir of their meeting, Mr Bush had gifted Britain's booksniffy, unchummy new prime minister who didn't do casual and was clearly ill at ease with displays of hairy machismo with a brown leather bomber jacket trimmed with a World War Two fur collar. It had a black name tag with 'Rt Hon Gordon Brown' printed in gold on the left breast and a Camp David badge with the presidential seal on the other. The jacket was identical to the one Bush himself had worn when he stood on an aircraft carrier thirty days into the Iraq war to declare 'mission accomplished'. (Identical to the one he had given Tony Blair, which Blair, 'tart that he is', as one commentator wrote, had been seen clambering aboard a helicopter in.) A quote from an aide that Brown 'wouldn't be seen dead' in his had to be hastily, and shamefacedly, contradicted.

On 31 July, the day he arrived home from the Camp David press conference, Brown had to be content to share the front pages of most of the broadsheet papers with news of the death of one of the cinema greats. Reading the tribute pieces and obituaries of Ingmar Bergman, who had died on his private island of Fårö, off the coast of Sweden, aged eighty-six – son of a strict Lutheran pastor whose sermons he had to inwardly digest every Sunday at all his father's Sunday services, a stranger to fashion, often derided for stiffness, for miserablism, for elitism and high seriousness – it was impossible not to be reminded of the son of the manse whose folded Shar Pei features glowered out of the same pages.

In the *Guardian*, Peter Bradshaw nominated *Winter Light* as Bergman's greatest film. It was, he wrote, 'in some ways the perfect title for a Bergman film with its connotations of severity, of purity, of religious observance'. Winter light was probably 'the light that he saw all around him on the remote island of Fårö where he made his home, very,

very different from the sensuous, exciting, neon-ish kind of light that it is Hollywood's business to convey.'

Wasn't this just another way of describing the sea-change that everyone sensed had happened in British life in just the few weeks that the Blair era of bling and flash briefings had given way to Brown's boiled grey woollen socks and strict moral compass? His brusque rejection of the notion of supercasinos and his predecessor's seriously relaxed attitude to drink and recreational drugs and all the devil's works? Just another way of saying – as John Kampfner had – that the old bank manager had returned, just when we had all lost hope of ever talking to one again?

'Winter light'. It described the gloomy English summer of morning mists and afternoon hail, the high winds and driving rain lashing Royal Ascot and Glastonbury, making a wash-out of the Season.

'A glass-half-full man, not a glass-half-empty guy' is how Bush had described Brown. It didn't feel like that, with what the Met Office called 'major rainfall events' creating virtual villages of caravan-land all across the country and dark warnings of a credit crunch and the coming global economic turmoil and more terror attacks expected. And the smile. The wintering smile. The lonely vigils among the teetering piles and dusty boxes in Cowdenbeath high street.

The clunking fist becoming the quivering wrist. From Stalin to Mr Bean in such a brief season. The grinning faces on the benches opposite. The laughter gusting down the aisles from the reptile enclosure.

The fall of great personages from high places, wrote George Steiner, gave to medieval politics their festive and brutal character. They made explicit the universal drama of the fall of man.

What would John Smeaton do?

Chapter Six

That weather-bloated summer – the monsoon summer, Britain's wettest summer on record, 48,000 homes and 7,000 businesses ruined, the most prolonged rainfall for 250 years – a new word was put into circulation which, in retrospect, would help capture its flavour: bowser. *A bummer of a summer.* Newsreaders started delivering bulletins about bowsers, the prime minister was said to be concerned about bowser-distribution, and bowsers provided a variety of ways for wide-boys and chancers to scam their neighbours, a tiny new spin on the multifarious ways of human malevolence and ingenuity.

Bowsers were portable tanks containing drinking water for areas whose supplies had been cut off by the floods. Army lorries dropped them off at emergency centres and on street corners. People with pots and buckets and battered plastic bottles that had once contained cider or Coke queued up to carry water home, suburbs of Cheltenham and Oxford become outposts of Bangladesh and Bihar.

But then people with industrial-size two- and four-gallon containers started turning up and loading the boots of their cars and driving away. There were scuffles, some with a racist undertow. There were reports of people opening the bowser taps under cover of darkness and leaving the water to drain away; others of people urinating in them to make the water undrinkable and the flood victims so desperate for tap water they would be prepared to buy it.

In parts of Yorkshire, Gloucestershire and the Midlands nearly two months' rain fell in a day. Reservoirs, brooks, rivers, drainage channels burst their banks. All-night watches were set up on some streets and estates to protect bowsers and scare away car thieves and looters. A large woman interviewed on the evening news in Quedgely outside Gloucester said she had been standing guard over the water supply since six in the morning. There was panic-buying; supermarkets reported an unprecedented run on bottled water. The causes of the floods were both global – global warming, of course, climate change, the melting of the polar ice-sheets, ice-sheets, ice-sheets, the rise of carbon emissions causing sea levels to rise – and local: villages built beside land that would normally act as a floodplain, straightened rivers, intensive farming, the destruction of places where water could once be temporarily stored, the widespread concreting-over of naturally absorbent land surfaces – tarmac drives, impermeable patios – and the disconnection of rivers from their floodplains.

All water has perfect memory and is forever trying to get back to where it was, Toni Morrison said once. It made

Britain prone to flash floods. And, sure as the Severn wanted to get along Westgate to the doors of the cathedral in Gloucester, and the salt sea wanted to reclaim Dave Bolger's house in Brixham (Mr Bolger, 68, collapsed and died as he struggled to pile sandbags in the porch against the floodwaters invading), the floods all translated into stories, a patchwork narrative of hardship and personal suffering, the revulsion at homely things turned unhomely, the familiar turned on its owners, themes of anxiety and dread – the plug of the shower in the en suite spewing sewage, first the noise, the thick nasty gurgling, and then the smell; the soil pipe exploding into the bedroom; the airbricks oozing worms, fish, who knew the rank tonnage of human waste; the receding deluge leaving in its wake acres of stinking, stagnant sludge.

There were polite ways to say it. Despoliation. Cloaca. 'The primal muck of dissolution'. And ways that were more vulgar: strangers' turds floating in your kitchen, tampons, toilet paper. And it was ongoing: an Environment Agency official said he worried about contamination, 'people shitting in plastic bags, and how we get rid of all that'.

Tony went and Gordon came, and it was a world in the throes of drastic and probably ominous transformation. A wet world; change taking place helter-skelter, without purposeful direction; an unsettling loss of agency.

'Since the First World War Americans have been leading a double life, and our history has moved on two rivers, one visible, the other underground; there has been the history of politics which is concrete, factual, practical and unbelievably dull . . . and there is a subterranean river of untapped, ferocious, lonely and romantic desires, that concentration of ecstasy and violence which is the dream life of the nation.' – Norman Mailer, 'Superman Comes to the Supermarket', *Esquire*, 1960.

Spring had arrived early: it was May in January, August in April, the sun a big yellow duster, the seasons flipped. Small wonder nature's creatures and the contents of her larder were confused. It was confusing times, especially if you happened to be a peacock butterfly or a longhorn beetle.

On 1 September, which they said was the first day of autumn, the *Independent* ran a front-page illustration – it was like a colour-plate from the schoolbooks of olden times, the times in which Gordon Brown had come of age, when the inherent superiority of high over low culture was taken to be a given – showing the species of wildlife that had been (this was the headline) the casualties of summer.

They included lapwings and bitterns that had their nests washed away; grey partridge, whose chicks had starved and frozen; water voles, drowned in their burrows, and the buff-tailed bumblebee, whose underground nests had been flooded out. The implications were serious. It was feared that the effects of the floods could turn out to be as serious as 1963 and the twentieth century's worst winter, when millions of wild creatures died in a landscape that was snowbound for two and a half months.

In 2007, nectar was washed away and pollen water-logged, a horror show for insects which feed on flowers. The slug population, on the other hand, doubled. By September, the country was witnessing a mosquito explosion. A resident of east London was quoted as saying that 'It's like Borneo in my bedroom.' A spokesman for the Zoological Society of London told the *Guardian*: 'The weather could be coming round to favour mosquitoes in a big way, and if we have more mosquitoes, we can probably expect an increase in the diseases they carry.' This meant myxomatosis in rabbits; malaria, encephalitis and dengue fever in humans. The aedes species of mosquito carries chikungunya, a highly debilitating disease causing fever, headaches and severe joint pain, which in 2006 devastated the French island of La Réunion, affecting 50,000 people. The culex mosquito transmits West Nile fever, known to have caused 600 deaths in parts of the United States over the past four years.

The drastic impact on habitats. The psychic damage to earthlings and their dependants, van-dwellers and waders through shit, exposed to the knowledge that torrential surface run-off, impermeable surfaces regulation and all this – every household to prepare a freakin 'flood kit' consisting of (inter alia) personal documents, torch, battery radio, rubber gloves, wet wipes or similar – all it really means is being brought face to face with the fact that the isle is full of beastie-weasties and creepy-crawlies, things that gorge on shite and lead slimy, hidden existences in the dung and the dark underwater, reaching out, those turbid germ-infected waters, trying to draw them down, to suck them under, the bastard indifference of nature to us and all our arrangements.

The fact that the natural world, even in the heart of the city, wrote Robert Alter, harbours a pullulation of inchoate, alien life irresistibly asserting itself against the neat geometric design of the urban planners. The flood-water animated as a formless primordial beast, seething and shrieking and lapping at the granite foundations of the city.

The relationship between the floods and the outbreak of foot-and-mouth at a farm in Surrey in August seemed at first (and so it was proved) to be a causal one. The farm was the near-neighbour of a government laboratory and a drain from the laboratory carrying live FMD virus could have fractured and spilled it into the ground. Areas of the farm had been flooded and foot-and-mouth can be water-borne. If flood water had been the cause, it would most likely have been a failure in treating effluent from the vaccine laboratories handling the foot-and-mouth virus, three miles away.

Again, reading these reports of the new outbreak of FMD and its likely connection with the floods, of the lapse in biosecurity measures that probably led to it, the sense of a subterranean secret life asserting itself, of it being stirred and flushed into the open.

It was just over a year since Hurricane Katrina and the devastation of New Orleans, and images of that catastrophe were still fresh in the memory. Prisoners from the

New Orleans jail herded onto a ramp of the collapsed and flooded freeway. The showpiece Superdome flayed by the storm and transformed overnight into an overcrowded and insanitary shanty town. The impoverished and the elderly lined up along a central reservation of a flyover awaiting evacuation eight days after the hurricane hit.

They added to the heightened sense of a loss of control, of being surrounded by menacing and perhaps inscrutable entities.

One teatime a man came on *Richard and Judy* to offer helpful tips and advice to anybody who might find themselves, like so many thousands had across the country, inundated by floodwater in their homes. Some of his hints were preventative and commonsensical: higher pedestals for cabinets in the kitchen, electric points higher up the walls, a bilge pump in the floor-space. And then, quite without warning, his down-to-earth, bluff, DIY persona darkened and the nightmare vision of death down bottomless pits and premature burial was unleashed into the living room and the Baby Belling world of caravan-land. 'If you have a manhole cover nearby,' he suggested, 'place an old car battery or heavy stone on it. It can blow out and float away and, once it's underwater, anybody could disappear into the hole.'

On 25 June, parts of Hull were washed away in the most devastating floods in the city's history. Just before ten that morning the leader of the council declared a 'major incident', an emergency planning term requiring special arrangements to be put into place, and quickly. An incident room was set up in the Guildhall and all non-essential council staff deployed across the city to sandbag buildings and close roads. Ennerdale sports centre in the north of Hull was designated an official rest centre (until it was itself flooded) to accommodate people who were beginning to abandon their homes and offices. The emergency services reported that the city was being overwhelmed.

Around ten-thirty, Michael Barnett who was twenty-eight and worked at 'Kingston Koi' in Astral Close, Hessle, in Hull, had started trying to clear debris from a storm drain behind the shop when his leg became stuck. Undaunted by water on account of working surrounded by water and the silky, banner-like movements of the nishikigoi, in English champion-grade carp, he had cleared the same drain in a previous flood just the week before. The cover had drifted away and been replaced by lengths of municipal railing bent into an improvised cage shape. It was this his leg had got wedged in up to the thigh and he was held there neck-deep in the fouled flood water as the emergency services struggled for four hours to lever or lift him free.

Michael worked closely with koi, which comes from the Japanese, simply meaning 'carp'. It includes both the dull grey fish and the brightly coloured varieties. Koi are symbols of love and friendship in Japan. They have been known to live to a great age and come to recognise the person that feeds them; they can be trained to come to the surface to take food from the hand and will gently nibble the tips of the fingers of their regular feeder. Koi and tattoos of koi are traditionally considered lucky in Japan.

Koi are cold-water fish. The water was cold even though it was nominally summer and, despite the best efforts to save him, rescue workers desperately trying to keep his head above water, amputation of the leg a constantly reviewed possibility, acetylene equipment sent for, a surgeon standing by, Michael was held by his leg in the dirty water and was slowly dying of hypothermia.

The pond is located far deep among the mountains of Mino Province. The locality is called Oppara, Higashi-Shirakawa Village, Kamo County (writes Dr Komei Koshihara, President of Nagoya Women's College, radio broadcast to the whole Japanese nation over the NHK radio station, 9.15 p.m., 25 May 1966). Nearby there are rustic hot springs called Oppara-onsen. Facing south towards the Pacific on the top of Mt Ontake, you will look down upon the locality at the foot of the mountain. Through the locality runs the Shirakawa, a tributary of the River Hida which again is the upper reaches of the River Kiso. A stream of limpid water never ceases to flow all the year round. It is this water that flows into the pond in which 'Hanako' lives and which was carefully constructed with stones in former days. Besides that, pure water trickled from the foot of the mountain streams close by into the pond, making the favourable conditions still more favourable. The pond cannot be called large, only being about five metres square.

'Hanako' is a nishikigoi, a special carp which a scientist, with the use of a light microscope, has found in 1966 to be 215 years old. All six carp that live in the pond of Dr Koshihara's native house in Gifu are found to be in excess of 140 years old. Dr Koshihara continues:

> You can see carp everywhere, but this red carp of ours, 'Hanako', you will be surprised to know how precious an existence she is. There did not exist in this world any such country as the United States of America yet at the time when this carp was born. It was 25 years later that America made public the Declaration of Independence in 1776. It is very interesting to think that during the long years that this carp has continued to live, a country by the name of the United States of America came into existence and has built up her present culture of high standard. To speak in Japanese fashion, it was born in the 1st year of Horeki, that is, in the middle of the Tokugawa Era. Please consider how long her life is, surviving the shogunate and later the national advancement of Meiji and Taisho, and still continuing to live to this day of Showa.
>
> This 'Hanako' is still in perfect condition and swimming about majestically in a quiet ravine decending Mt Ontake in a short distance. She and I are dearest friends. When I call her saying 'Hanako! Hanako!' from the brink of the pond, she unhesitatingly comes swimming to my feet. If I lightly pat her on the head, she looks quite delighted. Sometimes I

go so far as to take her out of the water and embrace her. At one time a person watching asked me whether I was performing a trick with the carp. Although a fish, she seems to feel that she is dearly loved, and it appears that there is some communication of feeling between us. At present my greatest pleasure is to go to my native place two or three times a month and keep company with Hanako.

Dr Koshihara concludes:

Our urban life has become, and is increasingly, dreary owing to the soiled atmosphere and noise. What do you say to making your daily life somewhat more enjoyable by constructing a pond for fancy carp? It can be done with only a little spare time and small labour. I call fancy carp 'Live Jewels', and I am convinced that they truly deserve the name. Thanks to their owner's loving care, the carp, male and female, grow larger and larger day by day. If you put your hand into the water they will gather around and suck the finger tips. It is to be sincerely desired that we all should have the spare time and self possession to stroke and pet these 'live jewels' on the back from time to time. Thank you for your kind attention.

Michael's father had gone to the culvert where his son was trapped. The owner of 'Kingston Koi' had telephoned him. Michael had worked there for twelve years, from leaving school, a talking textbook on koi. Police officers kept his father back and advised him that he should either stay in a police car or go home. As he watched television, he heard 'that the young man trapped in the drain had died'. He then waited for a number of hours for police to come and confirm what had happened.

Did Michael imagine he could feel his favourite nishikigoi using its mouth to caress the tips of his fingers as consciousness ebbed? That it was Ghost koi, the modern metallic hybrids, at play around his feet, stirring the substrate, increasing the brown turbidity of the water, rather than contaminating slime and human effluent? I'd like to think so. A stream of limpid water never ceases to flow all the year round. It is this water that flows into the pond in which Hanako lives.

The solidity of the external world dissolved. The feel of life in this new waterlogged reality.

Astral Close.

Some say the drains are heaven's guts.

Chapter Seven

1 tub, Sudocrem – 1 'Taste the Difference' butter-roasted chicken salad sandwich – 1 tub, 'Taste the Difference' coleslaw (was 96p now 50p) – 2 bottles Caledonian sparkling natural mineral water – 1 Madagascan vanilla Jersey milk yogurt (was 59p now 25p) – 1 Fruits and Nuts ('a luxurious mix of nuts and juicy fruits')

He didn't know why he made this list of everything he had just bought from the late shop whose lights he could still see spilling into the village from his upstairs window. The Sudocrem was to draw the heat out of the sunburn he had suffered on his face and scalp. The forecast had been rain, more rain. The forecast was wrong. The afternoon had brought strong sun and he had toiled up the hill between the Trimdons like an old Chinaman, thinking (too late) to use his pocket-size umbrella with the broken spoke as a sun-shade, tilting it to obscure his face every time a car approached on the near side. Maybe he saw the list as a diary – a displacement diary of the depredations of being away from home.

He knew writers had to travel away from home sometimes in order to gather material – it was part of the writer's life. But he always fell avidly on writers writing about their (preferably fed-up and futile, preferably seedy) on-the-road existences. He often went back, for instance, to Naipaul's tender description of his eighteen-year-old self, spending his first night in a New York hotel, on his first night away from his island. He has with him half a roasted chicken that his family, at the ritual family farewell, has pressed on him at the airport, thousands of miles away and many hours earlier. 'I ate over the waste-paper basket, aware as I did so of the smell, the oil, the excess at the end of a long day . . . like a man reverting to his origins, eating secretively in a dark room, and then wondering how to hide the high-smelling evidence of his meal. I dumped it all in the waste-paper basket. After this I needed a bath, or a shower.'

Of the many descriptions of the erotic possibilities of down-at-heel hotel rooms in Graham Greene, he particularly remembered the one from *England Made Me* about Minty, the expatriate freelance hack: 'The room was cold . . . it was bare. He tore the coloured cover off an old *Film Fun* and stuck it against the wall with a piece of soap . . . He tore out a picture of Claudette Colbert in a Roman bath and balanced it on his suitcase. Two girls playing strip poker he put above his head with more soap.' The older Greene, he knew – the established, mysterious, debonair writer – always stayed at the Ritz on his visits to London. But he preferred to think of the younger man in some bare and shabby rented room, like the character in his novel, arranging his trousers under the mattress before turning in, to press the creases in them.

Only the day before, on the train travelling north from King's Cross to Darlington en route to Sedgefield where the by-election to pick Tony Blair's successor was about to take place, he had come across a story which he sensed even before he had read a whole page was going to become one of those pieces of writing he would return to when he wanted to be reminded of the special pleasures as well as the privations of being in a strange place, following a story. 'A man likes to be alone sometimes. Being alone doesn't mean being where there are no people. It means being where people are all strangers to you.'

Idly flipping through the pages, at the same time watching the colours of the countryside go by, those words had instantly drawn him in and made him go back to the start of the story.

Looking for an excuse to put aside the various press releases and printouts going over the issues in the Sedgefield campaign (it was a non-campaign – there was no way that Phil Wilson, the Labour candidate and a longtime confrère of Blair's, wasn't going to win, and he couldn't pretend that the state of Newton Aycliffe health centre or the regeneration of Aycliffe town centre held any real interest for him, any more than they had for Tony Blair, who had appeared to do nothing about them in his twenty-four years as MP), he had opened a paperback book of stories by Sherwood Anderson that he had had for several years but had never looked at until then. The lines that trapped his eye were from a story called 'In a Strange Town', which he worked out had been written around eighty years earlier by a writer who had always had to live in the shadow of Hemingway and Fitzgerald and his friend William Faulkner. It didn't seem so old. It still seemed fresh, with romantic unpoetic sentences that rang with an arresting off-note.

'A morning in a country town in a strange place', it started. 'I have come away from home. I am in a strange place'.

Slowly he read on, no longer agitated by the over-amplified customer announcements before and after every 'station-stop'. No longer anxious that the trip was going to turn out to be a waste of time and money and tell him nothing about Blair he didn't already know, or apprehensive about where he was going to end up spending the night. Bright colour seen from the train that went to Darlington.

> I will sit in this hotel until I am tired of it and then I will walk in strange streets, see strange houses, strange faces. People will see me. Who is he? He is a stranger.
>
> That is nice. I like that. To be a stranger sometimes, going about in a strange place, having no business there, just walking, thinking, bathing myself. To give others, the people here in this strange place, a little jump at the heart too – because I am something strange.

Having made the list of items picked up from the late shop, next he felt he should add a description of the room where he was going to be for several nights (fewer nights than he told the man at the desk he was going to be staying – not hanging around for the count at the leisure centre, not even waiting for by-election day itself, he would bail out on day three) in case at some time in the future he should need to recall the details. It was a pub room of the kind he had stayed in all too often: stencilled dado line of green leaves and orange flowers, brought round slightly higher on one side of the doorframe than the other; small dusty Japanese-made television, missing the remote; cheap boxwood furniture stained coffin-like dark mahogany brown, with rust-mottled shiny gold hinges and handles; a loose-grouted tile on the floor in the bathroom which rocked every time you crossed to the sink. The only unusual feature was the windows which, from the outside, could be seen to be half the height of the traditional sash windows on the two lower floors. The room he had been given was at the top of the building and extended into the pitch. The windows in both bedroom and bathroom came up only as high as his waist and he had to bend like the giant peering into Goldilocks' house to see through either.

That first night, as he sat on the edge of the bed eating his butter-roasted chicken salad sandwich and 'Taste the Difference' coleslaw, he looked up condolence messages and tributes on mydeathspace.com and gonetoosoon. co.uk, impressed as always by the way ordinary keyboard symbols like +'s and ( )'s could be turned into representations of angels' faces and bouquets of flowers, absorbed by the gap between the obviously genuine sentiments of many messages – 'still to dis day i fink 2 myself y, y u but ima cum c u soon bruv, nuff love' – and the texting shorthand they were expressed in; trying to decipher the lyrics of the rap songs that came on as the soundtrack to the details of many violent young deaths connected with petty crime and drugs and run-ins with the police and all the stuff of proletarian outsiderdom – lyrics he had a tin ear for.

'Well, alright!' is something he knew the young Blair, a Jagger fan, did a lot of during his few appearances as the singer with Ugly Rumours, the band he joined while he was studying law at Oxford in the early Seventies. 'Well, alright! . . . I said, Well, alright!' This – catastrophically – was Neil Kinnock's attempt to show that he was youthful, modern, dynamic and 'down with the kids', leaping onstage at Labour's famous 'pre-victory' election rally at Sheffield Arena in spring 1992, shortly before they were humiliated at the polls by John 'warm beer, invincible green suburbs, dog lovers and pools fillers, old maids bicycling to communion through the morning mist' Major.

In addition to sending him to Nicki Clarke, hairdresser to the stars, for a style re-think and putting him into 'softening' fuchsia ties in the period leading up to his coronation, part of 'Project Gordon' had been to get him to boast in public about being a toe-tapping, hand-jiving Arctic Monkeys fan. In terms of street-credibility this ranked alongside Kinnock's stadium-rock shout-out and Blair's 'So what's the scene like out there?' to Damon Albarn the first time they were introduced, and ensured that Project Gordon was swiftly binned in favour of Plan A, the sober, statesmanlike sell.

The place he found himself staying was a former coaching inn with traditional lime-washed walls and black pointing and a deep arch that still opened on to a cobbled yard at the back of the building, and then open fields. The pub was part of a terrace running adjacent to the main road which acted as an effective baffle between Sedgefield village and the countryside around it. On one side were the tea-rooms and shops and pubs and the everyday commerce of the village, and on the other the woods and meadows; the Sainsbury's Local selling ready-meals and magazines until very nearly midnight, and in the darkness just beyond the light from its window, the natural habitats of bats and cinnabar moths and green-winged orchids come into flower two months ahead of time.

Part of the yard of the pub had been turned into a beer garden, with rickety-looking, rustically knocked-together furniture coated in black gloss paint; the arch, whose lower walls still bore the long scars of carriage axles, was used by smokers to stay out of the rain.

Next door to the pub was 'Minsters', a restaurant painted in the same traditional black and white colours where the Blairs could sometimes be seen and whose owner had done the catering for 'their Leo's' christening. Minsters was cosy and chintzy with satin-tasselled lamps and tassels dangling from the heavy, faux-leatherbound menus. It was on the main road and gave, local people felt, a good picture of Sedgefield. It was quiet, it was discreet; it was above the average pocket. This was the kind of place Sedgefield saw itself as being. It got their goat that outsiders confused their village, a market town since the fourteenth century that was sometimes described as looking 'as though it could be in the Cotswolds', with the larger Sedgefield constituency represented by the prime minister.

They took particular exception when visitors supposed that the famous Trimdon Labour Club, the setting for so many momentous Tony Blair occasions, had somehow something to do with them. For a start, they weren't Labour. Unlike the retired pit villages that were at the heart of the constituency, they weren't dyed-in-the-wool Labour; they were true-blue, dyed-in-the-wool Tories. Only the accident of a boundary line stopped them voting for that bonnie William Hague, just a few miles away in Richmond, in North Yorkshire.

The drug abuse and junkies, the crackheads and plonkies that other former mining communities in County Durham were now notorious for, the child neglect and glue-sniffing that was always getting written up in the papers – that had nothing to do with them. Tattooed tearaways. 'Cut here' written round their necks. Fishburn and

Trimdon Colliery, a few bus stops away, were like alien territory. And where was Blair's favourite pub? Always the clincher. It wasn't in Trimdon Village or Doggie or any of the Trimdons. It was the Dun Cow, here in the village, whose elderly owner could be spotted most mornings in his roomy army-surplus khaki shorts and open-toed sandals disappearing under the arch at the pub where he was staying, off for an outward-bound across the fields.

In common with most places that summer, the weather had killed the tourist trade. There was a gang of labourers in that he would hear tramping between rooms, horsing around at night. But by nine o'clock they had long gone and he was always the only one at breakfast.

By then – mid-July; the by-election was on 19 July – the smoking ban had only been in effect for a fortnight. The upholstery of the bench seats in the bar smelled strongly. They had soaked up smoke and nicotine over many years. They were sticky with it. There was a grease mark on the sugar bowl roughly the size of a thumbprint that would still be there next time he stayed; an area of dirt around the lip of the milk jug also seemed ingrained and indelible.

He was always given the same table – it was the one under the blackboard always chalked up with the same options – 'chips & gravy or curried sauce', 'chicken goujons & 1 dip (choice of chilli, bbq, garlic, marie rose)' – and waited on by the same person.

Breakfast service was the domain of a hefty youth, tall and well-padded as they say up there, prematurely balding and dimpled like a large grubby baby. He never saw him wear anything other than a grey sweatshirt with a dark grease stain stretching from just below his chin to just above his generous belly. It was certainly his fingerprints on the crockery.

The breakfast waiter was talkative and curious, forever hovering between the tables and his place in the kitchen, a limp tea towel in his hand, a knowing expression on his face. Like many men in the 'hard' north-east, he had a pronounced feminine, almost skittish, side to his personality.

He seemed intelligent and gave the impression that he might once have been the victim of bullies at school, which had held him back and explained this menial, low-paying position. He hated Blair: 'If I could, and I knew when he was coming, I'd tip off al-Qaida so they could come and get him,' he said one morning. He seemed disaffected with all mainstream politicians, and to think of himself as some sort of edgy, anarchistic figure. 'Politically deranged'. He liked this phrase. It was what Phil Wilson, Blair's anointed successor, had called him on his doorstep when he was canvassing one evening.

It was through the breakfast waiter, who enjoyed being a conduit for useful, sometimes mischievous, information, that he learned that Reg Keys, whose son had been killed in Iraq, had had his room for the three weeks of the 2005 general election, Blair's last.

Reg Keys had put himself up as an anti-war candidate to oppose Blair on his own doorstep. His son Tom was one of six redcap soldiers who had been murdered in a particularly brutal attack on a police station in Majar al-Kabir in Iraq in

2003. As no weapons of mass destruction were ever found, Reg Keys believed Tom had been betrayed by the government and died for a lie.

'If this war was justified then I would not be here today. If the war had been just I would have been grieving and not campaigning,' he said at Sedgefield after the 2005 count, where he polled 10 per cent of the vote. 'If weapons of mass destruction had been found in Iraq, then I would not have come to Sedgefield, to the prime minister's stronghold, to challenge him on its legality.' With both Blairs standing immediately behind him and all eyes on them (Cherie was widely believed to have opposed the war), he added: 'I hope in my heart that one day the prime minister will be able to say sorry to the families bereaved by this war; I hope in my heart that one day he will find himself able to visit in hospital the soldiers who have been wounded by it.'

On 27 June, the day he finally stood down as prime minister to make way for Gordon Brown, Jonathan Freedland noted in the *Guardian* that here was no hint of a leader made to dip his head for the 'fateful, lethal mistake' of Iraq: 'Unbelievably, he has choreographed his exit with a thousand send-offs: cheers at Sedgefield, a last hug at the White House, a final round of backslapping from European leaders last week, and yet another ovation from a Labour conference on Sunday.'

Freedland contrasted Blair's lack of contrition with Eden in the wake of Suez, Lyndon Johnson in the aftermath of Vietnam, prime minister Begin and the Lebanon war of 1982, 'all of them broken by the knowledge of the suffering and death their decisions had caused'.

Eight months after the invasion of Iraq in March, 2003 – five months after Tom Keys' death at Majar al-Kabir a few days before his twenty-first birthday – Tony Blair had invited George Bush to be his guest at Myrobella in Trimdon Colliery, and to lunch at the Dun Cow in Sedgefield. It was the first state visit by an American president in over eighty years and advance parties of FBI and CIA crawled all over everything for weeks in advance of Bush's arrival. On the day, Air Force One touched down at Teeside airport. The motorcade of twenty armour-plated limousines with outriders, the presidential mobile hospital, the president's personal surgeon, the full panoply of bomb-blast mitigation and mortar-spray protection made its way to Trimdon Colliery. After a tea break at the Blairs' house, the procession continued along the winding lanes, bypassing the worst eyesores of Ferryhill and Fishburn, to the pub lunch in Sedgefield.

The protesters had been corralled at Sedgefield race course. With their loudhailers and their banners, they were marched by the police in an orderly fashion into the village in time to vent their anger at the president and prime minister, who smiled and shook hands for the cameras a safe distance away on their side of the wide cordon sanitaire.

The publican at the Hardwick Arms nailed a notice to the door that day. It said: No Presidents, No Prime Ministers, No Press. 'They're always on about how do you "feel",' he said. 'What do you "feel" about . . . How did you "feel" when . . . It's none of their bloody business how I feel about anything. That notice wasn't put there as a joke. I told them haddaway. Gan piss up your kilt.'

Early doors, Paul Trippett said, it was exciting for every-body. But after Tony became prime minister, especially after 9/11, and even more so after Iraq, just getting him into the club for ten minutes became a major operation. The installation of Hardstaff concrete TVCBs, a familiar sight at airports, stations and anywhere else construed to be under threat from a high-speed car bomb, staff clearances, sniffer dogs . . . It got too dodgy, for security reasons.

Paul has always lived local. When he was younger he had a reputation in the village as a bit of a lad. Motorbike, blond hair down to here. He did his time as a joiner, and then was steward at Trimdon Labour Club for many years. Paul was one of the group of 'famous five' Labour activists who talented-spotted Blair back in 1983 and, instantly smitten, threw themselves into getting him selected to stand.

Paul's importance to the organisation was demonstrated on the day of the presidential visit, when he was seated between Blair and Bush for lunch at the Dun Cow. ('What was it he said when you asked him about Iran?' Tony whispered to Paul when the president was briefly out of earshot, pressing the flesh. 'Oh, that's between me an' George, Tony,' Paul replied.)

The first time he phoned Paul to ask for a meeting, he

was told that afternoon was difficult. He had on Ofsted report thing at the school in Trimdon, then he wanted to watch the European Cup qualifier between England and Russia at four, and after that he'd promised to take the grandbairns to the pictures. 'Sorry, mate.'

The night Blair had come knocking on John Burton's door to try to convince him that he was the right man for Trimdon there had been football on the telly and he had to wait to make his pitch until the match was finished, tie loosened, jacket off, showing his familiarity with the players' nicknames and protesting that that was never a yellow! C'mon, ref!

(On the night of his audition as the singer for Ugly Rumours, Blair had turned up at the lead guitarist's rooms at Corpus Christie in Oxford clutching a sheaf of neatly transcribed lyrics to the songs that made up the group's intended set: 'Live With Me' and 'Honky Tonk Women' by the Rolling Stones; Jackson Browne's 'Take It Easy'; 'Black Magic Woman' by Fleetwood Mac; 'China Grove' and 'Long Train Running', both by the Doobie Brothers; and Free's 'All Right Now'. 'Let's go, honeys,' according to John Harris, is something he was heard to say often in those days when he was in female company. In Gordo's days as a student politico at Edinburgh, meanwhile, his hotties went by the name 'Brown's Sugars', presumably all unaware of the cunnilingual and racial connotations of that particular Stones track.)

'Tony chose Labour. I was born Labour,' Phil Wilson said when he was elected to succeed Blair as MP. That was true of all the 'famous five' – Wilson, Paul Trippett, Peter Brookes, Simon Hoban and John Burton – who had gathered at Burton's house that night to watch the latest blow-in perform his dog-and-pony show for them.

Burton had become Secretary of the Trimdon branch of the Sedgefield constituency when it was reformed for the '83 General Election. He taught PE and history at Sedgefield Comprehensive and the four younger men had once all been his pupils. In these times of fanatics, of *madrasas* and creepy politico-religious indoctrination, it struck him that the Trimdon cell had something vaguely sinister or maybe cabalistic about it. The charismatic leader, his devoted followers, the cave redoubt in the tribal lands of the little-populated northern part of the country, the prayers, the plotting, the paranoia, the chants. We're in the magic mountains, where all the shadows have rainbows. Strange shapes from the magic mountain range. You read about these things in the papers.

Paul Trippett told him that he had in fact been to a weekend school on Holy Island that flew the banner of Labour Young Socialists but was actually a cover for Militant. There they were coached in what was known as 'entryism' – how to take over Labour branches and swing them to the hard left. Paul had sold copies of *Militant Tendency* at weekends in the shopping centre, spent week nights leafleting. A donkey jacket and lank metal-head hair. Dave Spart.

Phil Wilson had followed a similar path. He left school with two O-levels and ended up working in the Co-op at

Peterlee and as a civil service paper-pusher at National Savings in Durham.

'I came out of Militant,' Paul said. 'Militant wanted to fight Labour, and I wanted to fight Tories. I was the prodigal son returning, so there was never a problem with me.'

Paul and Phil had both just renounced extremism and begun to embrace the philosophy of a nicer, happier, kinder society that would be the hallmark of New Labour in the future and become fully paid-up members of the Labour party for a second time when opportunity, in the shape of the personable young public-school- and Oxford-educated barrister from London, came knocking. It seems they all sensed from the beginning that Tony was Cabinet material. And it seemed that Tony sensed that here at last was the tight little gang of proletarian tykes, a bit unfinished on the outside but hearts of gold underneath, that he had never had. 'Where we going, fellers?' 'To the top, Johnny.' 'To the top of what, fellers?' 'To the toppermost of the poppermost, Johnny!' It's about fellowship, friendship, brotherly love. 'One nation', 'the future not the past', 'renewal' were the buzzwords. The totalitarianism of the totally pleasant personality.

From the outside, it looked as if handing on Sedgefield, one of the safest Labour seats in the country, like the (some thought, scandalous) handing on of the prime minister's job on the bigger stage, was part of what the Americans know as a sweetheart deal (or palimony, in the case of Blair-Brown). In addition to any surrogate role he might have played in the constituency for Blair, Phil

Wilson had been employed at Number 10 and had also worked at Labour HQ at Millbank: he had been in charge of the 'Prescott Express' throughout the triumphant, Labour's-coming-home 1997 election, helping keep JP on an even keel by pumping the bus full of Billie, Ella, Basie and Sinatra, all the old Parky favourites (as well of course as reporting back regularly to Tony on the state of mind of a strategically important colleague who was nevertheless considered to be a bit of a loose cannon).

But in July, in the low-key run-up to the by-election in which there was only ever going to be one winner, everybody was telling him that no kind of sweetheart deal was ever offered, and none accepted.

Paul Trippett insisted that for two years they had had to be on their guard against plans Number 10 might have been hatching to parachute some young hotshot in. They had come up with a counter-plan of their own just in case. Internally, they referred to this as 'SCAB': Sedgefield Constituency after Blair.

The basic thought they started to plant in people's minds was that, after a decade of a virtually absentee Member of Parliament (which is how a significant minority of constituents regarded their celebrity PM), it was essential that the new MP be familiar with the area and be available to focus on all the meat-and-potatoes issues which inevitably in the Blair years had tended to be ignored. 'I'll go to all your fairs and fetes': this was Phil Wilson's solemn promise to all the people he was appealing to to get him elected.

Paul Trippett was going to give up his job running the Labour Club to become Phil Wilson's full-time office manager and political adviser after the election. They had grown up together. They were both schoolboys at the time of the Kennedy assassination and could never have dreamed that they would themselves one day be part of a kind of Camelot-at-the-court-of-King-Tony in their own tiny little corner of the north-east of England. It was a word that Paul brought up himself in conversation. 'When Camelot goes, like,' he would say, or 'With Camelot gone, as it were', looking ahead to life in the new SCAB era.

Tony was starstruck. He liked rubbing shoulders with Sir Cliff and Bono and Barry Gibb and gladly accepted invitations to make use of their rock-star mansions. He was reported to be sick with nerves before appearing at the Brits and overawed at the prospect of meeting Noel Gallagher. He was relentlessly mocked in the press for the calibre of the guests he had down for supper at Chequers: Vernon Kay and Jimmy Savile; this was hardly the Rat Pack. Charlotte Church. She was hardly Pablo Casals.

And yet, in his natural inclination towards MOR and his familiarity with the stars of the more hummable end of the light-entertainment spectrum, Tony was closer to JFK in many ways than the mockers supposed. The Kennedy White House only came to be known as 'Camelot' when Jacqueline Kennedy called in Theodore White, the journalist, for an interview just after her husband's death and revealed to him that the president liked to repair to their private quarters and play the Broadway show album, featuring the songs of Lerner and Lowe sung by Robert Goulet and Julie Andrews.

Cherie Blair of course came from a showbusiness background. Her father, Tony Booth, was not only a famous face on television, best known as the Scouser layabout son-in-law of Alf Garnett in *Till Death Us Do Part*, he was also what used to be known in those days as a well-known 'socialist firebrand'. ('Feckless' was a word also often used to describe him and, even in his anecdotage, is still sometimes used in connection with Tony Booth today. He was absent when Cherie married Tony in 1980, recuperating in hospital from the severe burns he had suffered in a drunken incident involving a five-gallon drum of paraffin, many bottles of Jameson's, and two members of the SAS.)

Kennedy went to Hollywood and spent time studying Gary Cooper and Clark Gable to try to work out what charisma was, how you got it and what it took to make it work for you. Tony had access to Tony Booth and he used him not only to pick up tips to improve his acting; he also used his father-in-law's very good contacts within the Labour party to get himself picked as the candidate for the Tory stronghold of Beaconsfield at a 1982 by-election.

The following year was Sedgefield, and he didn't hesitate to wheel on not just Cherie's father, but also Tony Booth's partner Pat Phoenix, who by that time had become indistinguishable to audiences from Elsie Tanner, the big earth-mother figure of *Coronation Street* who she had been playing for nearly a quarter of a century.

Like Tony Booth, Pat Phoenix was a lifelong Labour supporter. She had been on first-name terms with both Wilson and 'Sunny Jim' Callaghan, the last two Labour prime ministers. ('The sexiest thing on television,' Callaghan had called her, as he cuddled her close on the doorstep at Downing Street for the benefit of the cameras while Harold Wilson, pipe in hand, looked on prime-ministerially.)

Born Pat Pilkington in Salford, she was part of that first generation of English actors for whom a working-class background and a north-country accent were regarded as bonuses rather than as drawbacks which would exclude them from top-class work. Before landing the part of Elsie Tanner she had appeared in Sandy Powell comedies like *Cup Tie Honeymoon*, made by the Mancunian Film Corporation in a converted church in Dickenson Road, Manchester, and in some of the British kitchen-sink classics of the late-1950s such as *The L-Shaped Room*. (She had narrowly missed out on being cast as Alice Aisgill in the film of John Braine's novel of the new cut-throat culture of getting and spending in the West Riding, *Room at the Top*.)

'Thay's a lovely big baussant bugger.' This, from an elderly male admirer fighting through a crowd to get near her at some function, was the sort of thing she was happy to take as a compliment. 'It was truthful and it had acid in it,' she once said, condensing the secret of *Coronation Street*'s appeal into a single sentence. She learned to treat the collapse of her private and public personas, and the resulting confusion among the *Street* faithful, as only understandable.

'Any more of that flamin' shoving and I'll come among you and sort you all out – and don't think I'm not capable.' Paul Trippett was amazed by the split-second transformation from sweet smiling Miss Phoenix, doing her bit on the stump, getting the vote out for her Tony's Cherie's lovely Tony, to hatchet-faced Mrs Tanner. There had been no public announcement of her appearance at Wingate community centre at West Cornforth, the village always known locally, for reasons nobody alive could remember, as 'Doggie', but there were thousands milling around outside by the time she arrived.

The thronging crowd, the TV lights, the perplexing shiver of celebrity, the press scrum. They were the kinds of scenes that operation SCAB was now deliberately consigning to the past. Part of the dedicated process of erasure of TB, whose parades were now all gone by.

For many within the constituency he was just a celebrity. He was on the TV. They wanted to see him. Not over landlord problems or illegal immigrants or the hospitals or schools. They just wanted to step into the glow. They were exercising their democratic right. They had picked up the phone and voted for Jonny Regan from Trimdon and seen him come in as runner-up ahead of that lardarse Jade Goody, useless fucking object, in *Big Brother 3*. Jonny the fireman, man, canny lad, you'd knaa 'im, bit of a rough diamond, deein' panto an' aal that now thi reckon, yid recognise his mam, smart little woman, dad gets in the club, played there in his group with his brother a couple times for Blair and his cronies at some bliddy a-dog-is-not-just-for-Christmas-save-some-for-Boxing-Day bliddy chequebooks-on-the-table, snouts-in-the-trough shitehawk fucking function.

'We got it in people's minds: "Local man . . ." Man?' Paul suddenly remembered his PCs. 'I mean . . . a local *person.*'

The erasure of Blair and Camelot culture was just another erasure in an area whose history was full of erasures, wipings-out, disappearances. The decorative pulley wheel, painted baby blue, that stands at Trimdon Grange now, on Jonny Regan's doorstep, ever a favourite of TB's for sessions with the press, is a reminder of the black-on-black landscapes and the lives that were once lived in the dark, underground; a token of the mining past whose deep scars have been landscaped and reclaimed; swarded over; attractively concealed. Huge shafts crammed with plastic rubbish.

The Martyrdom of the Mines – an ancient image. Militant masculinity. Blood on the coal. 'Grimly honest' realist dramas in which, as Greene once noted, the colliery winding gear, silhouetted against the sky, the pit disaster and the warning siren became as cinematically familiar as the Eiffel Tower or the Houses of Parliament. Powerful symbols of the 'old Labour' heartlands from which Tony Blair had so successfully extricated his party.

The false teeth which could be pawned on the Monday and taken out on the Friday since there would be no fresh meat to chew on before Sunday roast came round. 'Nay,

Christ, bloody 'ell,' Jack Gillam, famous outspoken northern impresario, once cautioned the future Elsie Tanner, 'you can't go touring round the provinces with a name like Pilkington. They'll think you're selling sausages or summat. Now, what can we call you?'

The Third Way. The recognition that mass politics was becoming middle-class politics. A politics that abandoned the old ideologies and claimed none of its own. 'If the man hadn't been Labour,' Paul Trippett told him, 'he wouldn't have been with us.' 10 Years, 3 Elections, 1 Great Britain.

On the last Monday of the by-election campaign Jacqui Smith, the new Home Secretary, dropped in to show her support for Phil Wilson. A retired couple on the council estate at Trimdon Grange had been teed up to tell her about their worries with regards to the rowdy behaviour of local young people and she was going to be able to reassure them and the local press who were present that this was just the sort of anti-social behaviour that she and the government of Gordon Brown were determined to come down on like a ton of bricks.

This was all going to happen over a relaxed cup of tea and biscuits at 14.40 hrs. By 14.30, the press and police and officers of the Special Branch and a mobile unit and uniformed staff of 'Streetsafe: fighting the fear of crime' bristling with CCTV cameras and radio masts were all in place, and the lady and the elderly gentleman, Mr and Mrs Churchill, stuck their heads tentatively out of their door just in time to have two youths with the England three-lions legend tattooed on their chests (they weren't wearing shirts), and who just happened to be passing, scowl aggressively at them and splat out gobbets of spit from between their front teeth in unison.

Jacqui Smith was new in the job. The first-ever female Home Secretary, the youngest since Churchill nearly a century before, she had been in place almost exactly two weeks. In the first 48 hours she had had the fluffed terrorist car-bomb attacks in London and Glasgow. There had been the row over whether she had shown too much cleavage while making a statement in the Commons, miscalculating the angles of the overhead cameras.

In Trimdon she seemed nervous. She was wearing trousers and expensive-looking suede stilettos. The trouser-suit had become creased through sitting and the creases emphasised the curves of her belly and her bottom. She was wearing a pendant necklace that he became fascinated by, the play of light through the purplish glass droplet onto the chaffed-looking, slightly reddened skin of her chest. (She had stepped up to the plate, as everybody seemed to keep saying about everything that summer. This was the level of scrutiny now. Get used to it.)

Did this look like a woman who would give Morrissey's *You Are the Quarry* as her favourite album? He wouldn't have said so. There was perspiration on her upper lip. She was speaking as if she was reciting from a script.

Her discomposure, it turned out, was because the papers had a story. 'Home Sec. Smoked Dope'. This on the day Gordon Brown was due to announce his intention to toughen the law on cannabis and reverse the 2004 declassification of it from a Class B to a Class C drug. 'Smiths' fan Home Sec. is tit-flashing stoner'. How very far from the days of R. A. B. Butler and Sir Reginald Manningham-Buller!

'JJ' (Jacqueline Jill) was part of the 1997 intake. She was one of Blair's Babes. Standing behind her in the famous picture of the beaming young prime minister surrounded by a crush of most of his 101 fragrant female MPs, smiling, waving at the camera from the steps of Church House, is Fiona Jones, the newly elected Member for Newark.

The papers had had a story on her just two months into 2007. How she had died. Drunk herself to death. How she had had some kind of fall from grace, been shunned by the Party fixers, and disappeared into the bottle (vodka at home because it didn't smell, whisky at work where nobody seemed to mind drink on your breath). By the end, the former television presenter, a staunch Liverpool Catholic, was just drinking and sleeping, nursed by her husband and her two sons. 'It sounds odd, but sadly we had got used to that kind of thing,' Chris Jones, who blamed the heavy-drinking culture at Westminster for his wife's alcoholism, told journalists.

The troubled life and lonely death of a New Labour MP.

One day Paul Trippett was kind enough to offer him a lift to Spennymoor. He was in his new job. Phil Wilson was the new MP. This was Phil's car, Paul said. It was a grey

VW saloon, a heavy layer of dust settled on the dashboard, a fair amount of rubbish floating about. Phil let him use it during the week when he was in London. His own car was a clapped-out Vauxhall Omega with 42,000 miles on the clock. What he had to show for all the years spent close to the red-hot beating heart of power. He still lived in the same house, ex-council stock. 'I've never been one for a diary or owt like that.'

As they went along he talked about how the Trimdon Labour Club was going through bad days. He had been in danger of losing his job there till the Party bought it. A lot of the pubs up this way, he said, clubs and pubs, were on their arses. He blamed the smoking ban and all the outlets for cut-price booze and the rise of dinner parties – people eating in each other's houses, a recent phenomenon in the north-east – all of this trying out Jamie and Nigella recipes on each other and all this.

At Spennymoor, one of the old centres of County Durham's mining industry, they stopped in the main street opposite the town hall. Its sooty Victorian facade was brightened with many flower-filled baskets and an electronic sign whose red tickertape display advertised the next big attraction: 'The fabulous UK's No. 1 magician Paul Daniels and Debbie McGee – full show and dinner'.

'That's the entrance,' Paul said, nodding, 'but it happened up aheight'.

Soon after he was elected MP for Sedgefield at the 1983 General Election, Tony Blair was invited to a meeting, supposedly being held to celebrate his victory, at

Spennymoor town hall. This was where the selection meeting, at which he had emerged triumphant over the hard-left candidate, Les Huckfield, had taken place, and where the '83 count had been held. On an otherwise grim night for Labour – it was the Falklands election, the raising up of the Blessed Margaret, joy unconfined – he had made his victory speech there.

On the night of the celebratory Trades Council meeting he was asked to speak first. He faltered in the face of a hostile audience. He was then rounded on by Dennis Skinner, the letters of whose name spelled out on paper even look like bared teeth. Skinner let rip, accusing Blair of betraying socialist principles. The verdict was unanimous: Skinner did him in. 'The night we got done at Spennymoor' is still spoken of often among the Blair faithful. Tony had been humiliated, and he was furious, vowing that the bastards would never do that to him again.

'He had been humiliated one night,' Paul Trippett said, 'but for the next twenty years he ruled the roost. That steel down his backbone came from Spennymoor town hall.'

Half a mile up the hill from the town hall lies the home of Norman Cornish. There are pictures in the town hall painted by Norman Cornish up to half a century ago. 'Don't call me the pitman painter.' This quote from Cornish was used as a headline on an article he himself had written at least, what, thirty years go. Oh easy. It was dear to him because it was the first piece with his name on it to appear in a national newspaper. Turned down for a trainee position on the local paper, he had got on a bus the very next day and travelled to Spennymoor to interview Cornish, whose paintings of pit workers and pit-village life he had seen at the Stone Gallery in Newcastle.

As well as paintings and small, tabletop abstract sculptures, heavily derivative (he now realised) of Barbara Hepworth and Ben Nicholson, the Stone Gallery also sold handcrafted rings and cufflinks and bracelets, the kind of 'artistic' jewellery he associated with wine-drinking and sophisticated, metropolitan gatherings. The Mr Stone the gallery took its name from smoked cheroots and wore knitted ties and had an artistic ring with what looked like some kind of pebble in it on his little finger. He wore blue gingham shirts and dusty pink corduroy trousers slung low under his considerable belly.

It was the tension between the world of which Mr Stone was such a colourful and comfortable part and the life of labour represented in the Cornish paintings hanging on the gallery's hessian-covered walls, brass down-lighters pouring light on to them, paintings whose titles – *Late Shift*, *The Pit-road*, *Man Walking Dogs* – spoke directly to what was in them, that he now supposed was what had made him take the bus to Spennymoor all those many years ago. He hadn't got any of that into the piece, which mainly consisted of quotes, his contribution being merely to mitre them together to make the equivalent of a simple box or stool.

And here he was back again, for the first time since then. Norman Cornish was still alive; he had established that. And he was still living in the same house, an easy uphill walk from the small, down-at-heel town centre.

The man who answered the door was recognisably Cornish; an old man, of course – he had to be well into his eighties – but still straight-backed and lean, same frank appraising gaze, sharp cheekbones and wary, hawk-like profile.

And his wife Sarah, who he had made many sketches of as a young woman, doing domestic chores, knitting, bathing the children, she was still pretty; she said she didn't hear so well, but she hadn't shrunk or spread or taken on any of the characteristics of an infirm old person.

She was still pretty and he was still handsome. They looked like young people who had stood in time for a while and the signs of age were mere prosthetics that somebody from make-up would come in and remove at the end of the conversation. He worked out that he now was a decade older than Cornish would have been on the occasion of their first meeting to do the interview for the newspaper (which they used, but which at the time of the bus ride out to Spennymoor hadn't been commissioned. He might have lied about that).

He couldn't say what had brought him there; he didn't exactly know. And although they were polite and hospitable, it was obvious they didn't remember him; couldn't picture his bald head covered in the long dark hair of his earlier visit, his face without the jowls. The piece he had written as a first step to getting a start as a writer (using Cornish then as he was maybe using him again now) seemed to be missing from their scrapbooks and neatly organised collection of cuttings.

Cornish talked. He seemed to enjoy talking, only bringing Sarah in when he wanted to be reminded of a name or a date. Edward Street, Thomas Street, Bishops Close Street; the Waterloo, the Vane Arms, the Bridge Inn, the Newcastle Bar, the Traveller's Rest. Spencer's butcher shop, Brook's grocer's shop, Brook's dress shop, J. G. Teasdale's milk business, Byer's joiners and undertakers office. He still lived where he had been born and he spoke of the streets and shops and pubs of his childhood as though they were still there, which for him in a sense they were. They were certainly preserved in the paintings and drawings, which hung around them as they talked.

He was self-educated. He had joined the sketching club at the Spennymoor Settlement at around the same time he had gone down the mine. His father had taken him to his colliery to get him set on. The pit, called the Dean and Chapter, at Ferryhill, was nicknamed 'The Butcher's Shop' owing to the number of accidents there.

Phil Wilson, the new MP's father, had a similar tale to tell. He worked underground at Fishburn colliery for thirty-eight years, often wearing oilskins because of the wet. Also now in his eighties, he has three inhalers for his emphysema, and can't move a thumb after a lump of wood fell on it underground. 'With that background, you can't be anything but Labour,' Phil Wilson told the local paper.

Cornish didn't want to talk Blair or politics. He wouldn't be drawn. Consider the implications of a telegraph pole, he said instead. It grows on a hillside in perhaps Scandinavia, is cut down and brought here by sea; people apply creosote, replant it, and it takes on the hum of countless voices. When you come up from the pit your hands are sore. You are tired and when you look up at a telegraph pole it looks like a crucifix. This is the recurring image of his paintings.

His talk was of the past, as the places and people of his pictures were fixed in a world which had largely disappeared. 'I sometimes wonder whether somebody's trying to obliterate my life,' he had said. And yet the room in which they were sitting had a light and modern feel about it, with modern, curvilinear Scandinavian furniture and none of the heavy pieces that people their age normally filled their homes with. The paperback close to his chair was a Penguin Classics edition of Darwin's *Origin of Species* that he said his brother-in-law had given him and which he was reading. The surfaces weren't cluttered with embrocations and elastic bandages and rows of pills. Beds hadn't had to be brought downstairs.

And yet it slowly emerged that there had been some recent scares. 'You know why she's left the room, don't you?' Cornish said at one point. 'It's because she can't stand hearing me talk about my health.'

On her return, settled again by the fire, necessary because of the prolonged damp and cold, Sarah too said that just this past year she hadn't been feeling herself. She shook her head. And he could see then what hadn't been obvious before; that, youthful-looking though they were, and though they lived in this big house scoured with light, pictures of the grandchildren in the fire alcove, they were beginning to envisage the end, and they were scared. One didn't want to be left behind without the other. There were flickers of irritation when either allowed their frailty, and therefore their age, to show, and a moving sense of fear.

After years working as a coal-hewer, bent double in the dark, using pick, shovel and drill, recent talk about soundings and scans had been giving him nightmares in which he was confined in tunnels, unable to move or think.

Before he left, Norman invited him to take a look in the studio. It was on the first floor in a big room over the kitchen, up a broad flight of stairs. The studio was dominated by a large painting-in-progress of one of his favourite subjects: men in a bar. It was a bar of the Fifties or even earlier: all the men wore hats – some trilbies, but mainly flat caps – and were sunk in a deep nicotine fug, refugees from the kingdom of toil.

The ease of association, the unselfconscious physical contact between the men was, as always, a notable feature. Arms were thrown across shoulders, heads leaned into heads, confidentially, all but touching. He was always fascinated by men standing at a bar drinking and talking, or sitting playing dominoes; the shapes they made; the gestures of mutual support.

There was the Irish Nyuk, where the Catholics sat. The Pigeon End for the pigeon men. Spongers' Corner. People used to take food to the pub on a Sunday – bowls of whelks, big bull whelks as big as your hand – pigs' trotters, hard-boiled eggs.

In an early entry in his diaries of the Blair years, Alastair Campbell writes: 'TB said in the end there are big people and little people. The big people do big things and the little people do little things.'

TB was a big person and he had a big project, changing the course of a country. Now that project was over, and the sense of disturbance that had invariably followed him north like a personal neurosis or a miasma, like a plough behind a tractor, turning over the world in its wake, could be allowed to settle and flatten out; local people could go back to concentrating on the little things that made their lives particular, and the locality could return with some relief to itself.

There was a hole in the landscape that, as in the recent past of the flash and dust and danger and noise of men at work, men at work around the clock, would soon be filled.

For the hole only gaped, wrote Zengotita of a bigger obliteration, in virtue of superimposed memory of a presence in that space, a space which (you couldn't help but notice) took up so tiny a fraction of the vastness of the wide horizon and the great bowl of the heavens above, so tiny a fraction of that vastness across which you cast your eyes whenever you looked away, a vastness into which that smoke was rising, so tenderly, until it dispersed at last into the brilliant blue.

The real focus of Cornish's composition was an amber

pint in a straight glass lightly beaded with sweat on the humanly patinated corner-turning of a bar. A pint of beer is a lovely convivial colour, he said. When I see a pint, I can see a man's hand lifting it.

Small pleasures, a lost world memorialised in the work of Cornish.

That ends this part of the story.

Chapter Eight

He woke in the night and went to the cabin-like room where he worked; it was book-lined, snug; he liked being there when the rest of the world slept. His wife was sleeping on the other side of the wall in the bed he had just left, the dog, released from its place in the kitchen, already wrapped in and groaning contentedly, foetally, in the space behind her knees.

In 1995 he published a novel called *Fullalove* that he hadn't opened in years. It took him several minutes – the need to find it suddenly seemed urgent – to locate a copy of the original hardback, stacked in a pile. It had a little dog on the cover, soft and cuddly, a child's comforter, like 'Cuddle Cat'. 'Fullalove' was the (fictitious) manufacturer's name, printed on a label sewn into the seam and taken from one of the 'dirty toy' pieces by the American artist Mike Kelley he liked very much. Called 'More Love Hours Than Can Ever Be Repayed', the title seemed to be both a reference to the love the child lavishes on the toy, which can be measured in the amount of wear and tear, the food and saliva and goo stains flattening the plush of the synthetic fibre, and the love the toy returns.

He opened the book and began reading. The narrator is a tabloid journalist, jaded, borderline alcoholic, self-hating, specialising in crime. A soft toy (the little dog), entrusted to him by the wife of the murderer of a young child which he had promised to place on the roadside memorial to the little girl but kept, is his only comfort and companion. Miller, the narrator, has also listened obsessively for some years to an audio-cassette of Meryl Streep reading the children's story *The Velveteen Rabbit*, and extracts from the story punctuate the narrative.

He started to remember the voice. He started to recall bits of the book he had forgotten: Shane Norwood, the nine-year-old stolen from his bedroom in south London by a stranger; Sean Norwood, his father, who had transformed personal tragedy into something positive by becoming a game-show host on daytime television; the ritual at the end of every show of the contestants waving 'Goodbye, Shane!' (he was still missing; no body had ever been found) to a big illuminated picture; the heartlessness and venality of the hacks covering the case.

The reason he had been awake, unable to sleep, was that his mind was racing, making connections. The previous day, Paul McCartney's wife – 'Lady Mucca' as the tabloids had taken to referring to her – had gone live on breakfast television with a tearful outburst against the press, who she said were hounding and relentlessly vilifying her and making her life intolerable. She described herself being in as much pain as Princess Diana 'and Kate McCann'.

In the 1960s, when it was still a fishing village and many miles off the tourist track, before the tiny harbour had become hemmed in by apartment blocks and resort hotels such as Mark Warner's Ocean Club – Paul McCartney had spent two weeks on holiday in Praia da Luz. It caused the kind of media scramble not seen again in Praia until May 2007. But, away from the barricades of Paris, Prague and London, 1968 was a simpler, better-natured time and, after McCartney had posed for pictures on the beach on the morning the papers first tracked him down, they kept their promise, went off happy with what they'd got, and left him in peace to enjoy the rest of his holiday. Fans brought gifts of soft toys and other presents and laid them respectfully outside the house where he was staying.

It was the first time Paul and Linda had gone away anywhere on holiday together. It was a spur-of-the-moment thing. Exercising some of the new-found power that the Beatles money which was just starting to cascade in was giving him, he had chartered a plane and, with Linda and Heather, Linda's daughter from a previous relationship, had flown down to Faro in the middle of the night.

Hearing pebbles rattling against a window was the first time Hunter Davies and his family, who had rented a converted sardine factory in the village for six months, realised that they had visitors. Hunter had just finished his biography of the Beatles and had held out the offer of the sleepy little village in Portugal as a bolt-hole, not really expecting that any of them would take him up on it.

The Praia da Luz that existed then has been wholly

absorbed into the modern resort that EasyJet has made accessible to holidaymakers from all over Britain and Europe. In those days you saw lots of disabled and disfigured local youths and men in the streets of Praia, hobbling around on crutches. Portugal was fighting a disastrous colonial war in Angola, and these were the ones lucky enough to come back alive.

It was while they were in Praia da Luz that Paul asked Linda to marry him, around the time she first discovered she was pregnant with Mary, now a celebrity photographer like her mother. This was the beginning of the family which, if rumour was to be believed, had tried to talk their father out of marrying Heather Mills and, when the marriage collapsed in a vituperative and very public way, would lend him such conspicuous support against the claims of the woman who went on television to compare her pain to Kate McCann's (who some in the crackling blogosphere claimed 'looked like Heather Mills's twin sister').

Heather followed Gordon Brown – now saddled with the nickname 'Bottler Brown' after failing to call an autumn election, and falling fast in the polls – onto the GMTV sofa. Beforehand, some papers reported, she had cornered him in the Green Room and tried to get him to promise to back her campaign to make any newspaper apology as prominent as the offending article. She wanted him to see how she had been vilely and repeatedly handbagged by getting him to look at the scrapbooks bloated with Lady Mucca stories she was toting, like the bag-lady of media gulch. The McCanns, meanwhile, were said to be feeling sore that the prime minister, once their close ally, had, in light of their *arguidos* status, apparently dropped them.

After her GMTV performance, Heather's PR adviser Phil Hall, a former editor of the *News of the World*, announced that he was dropping her. Hall had previously been in discussion with the McCanns about the spokesperson's role which was eventually filled by Clarence Mitchell. Mitchell's predecessor in the job in Praia, Justine McGuinness, was currently working as special adviser to the beleaguered Lib Dem leader, Sir Ming Campbell. Another former editor of the *News of the World*, Andy Coulson, was working very effectively as David Cameron's Alastair Campbell, who was just then working on a lecture in which he would lambast media 'hysteria' over the McCann case, calling it 'the worst example of recent times of some newspapers thinking the word Madeleine sells, and finding literally any old nonsense to keep her name in that selling position on the front'.

With all this in his brain, he couldn't sleep. Bizarre links. Connections. (Kate McCann's parents, Sue and Brian, made their trips to Praia da Luz via Faro from John Lennon Liverpool Airport!) And then – propelled out of bed in search of the book he hadn't opened for many years – he saw at this late stage the glaring correspondence between the little dog fetishised by the tabloid reporter Miller in his novel (it was death-connected; it had been meant for the shrine to the murdered child; Miller had kept it) and Madeleine's plush pink Cuddle Cat, the talismanic link with her daughter carried everywhere by Kate McCann in the weeks following Madeleine's disappearance.

They had left her hugging Cuddle Cat on the night of 3 May when they went to join their friends (soon, like hostages or terrorists, to be known as the 'Tapas 7') for dinner. It was finding Cuddle Cat there and Madeleine missing that they said made them sure somebody had taken her. She wouldn't have gone anywhere on her own without Cuddle Cat. Madeleine and Cuddle Cat were inseparable, the soft pastel nylon pelt, the stuffing of polystyrene pellet mix and low-grade synthetic waste, the chocolate and sunblock and dribble stains, the smell of herself and Cuddle Cat the same, enjoined; the love hours, the expressionless, idealised, machine-made face, full of empty content, waiting to be filled. A tactile object to be sucked, squeezed, humped and drooled on until its last erotic delights had been yielded and it had become literally filthy.

'It is grubby now, a little battered and undoubtedly tear-stained,' began a report in the *Telegraph* a week after Madeleine disappeared.

'Generally, by the time you are Real, most of your hair has been loved off, and your eyes drop out and you get loose in the joints and very shabby,' the wise old Skin Horse tells the Velveteen Rabbit. 'But these things don't matter at all, because once you are Real you can't be ugly, except to people who don't understand . . . for nursery magic is very strange and wonderful, and only those playthings that are old and wise and experienced understand all about it.'

'I was desperately hoping that Madeleine would be back before the Cat got washed,' her mother told *The Times* on 8 August. 'In the end Cuddle Cat smelt of suntan lotion and everything. I forgot what colour it was.'

Mike Kelley has often said that 'dirt' is what his installations, consisting only of abject and orphaned cuddly toys picked up from yard sales and thrift-stores, are really about: 'Because dolls represent such an idealised notion of the child, when you see a dirty one you think of a fouled child. And so you think of a dysfunctional family . . . The toy begins to take on characteristics of the child itself – it smells like the child and becomes torn and dirty like real things do. It then becomes a frightening object because it starts to represent the human in a real way and that's when it's taken from the child and thrown away.'

In a society fuelled by pictures of success, wrote Ralph Rugoff, these images of failure generate the anxiety which surrounds the taboo. Kelley's creatures are not funny on account of their pitiable appearance, but because they befoul the sublime hygiene of the gallery or museum (or double-fronted executive dream home). Examine them too closely and their lovable personalities dissolve into clumps of unwashed fabric, limp and devoid of architectural structure.

After their flight from Praia da Luz in early September, the helicopter tracking shots at that end, the crate of toys in the driveway of the white adobe Vista do Mar, the helicopter tracking shots at this end, the paparazzi riding pillion, facing backwards to get the eyes of Gerry and Kate, the figures standing in sun-roofs, Richard Bilson outside apartment 5A at the Ocean Club resort, Huw Edwards in the studio, it was repeatedly reported that the Portuguese police wanted to re-examine – 'seize' was always the English translation – Madeleine's Cuddle Cat, on which the sniffer dogs had allegedly picked up 'the scent of death' in the summer.

Oh, he would have liked to switch off, crawl quietly back to bed. But his mind kept scratching away.

Their friends are the 'Tapas 7'.

We are in the auspicious year of 'Triple Seven'. 07.07.07. 'Three Sevens'. The phenomenon of the Triple Seven weddings. The best man getting up and saying exactly 777 words in exactly 7 minutes.

Seven is considered a lucky number in Western culture. A common winning line in simple slot machines. 7 Hills of Rome. 7 Wonders of the ancient world. The number of the 7 Virtues – chastity, moderation, liberality, charity, meekness, zeal, and humility – corresponding to the 7 Deadly Sins. The 7 terraces of Mount Purgatory (one per deadly sin). The number of sacraments in the Roman Catholic faith.

The number of colours of the rainbow. The number of spots on a common ladybird.

Nursery images which made him think of Kate McCann. Madeleine's room was pink. Sometimes she lies on Madeleine's bed. Sometimes in her own bed at night she wakes up and is sure Madeleine is there. 'Tormented Kate McCann is regularly woken up by visions of the 4-year old in her bedroom.' Copy filed with an implied catch in the voice, a muffled sob in the throat, sentimental as a lollipop.

When the time comes for the twins' birthday – they will be three – she decides she will send them cards from Madeleine, a lovely present from Madeleine, they still say 'And one biscuit for Madeleine' their big sister, invite all their friends, as if she was still there. Her Winnie-the-Pooh pyjamas. The blank-faced man.

The empty desk being saved for Madeleine. The head teacher of the school Madeleine would have gone to setting up an empty desk shrine with candle.

People crowd at the edge of the oddly regular weave of the blankets of flowers, stunned by the scale of what they have made. But soon they turn into just one more example of urban blight; of city sadness. 'A little angel lost in flight' is the sort of thing it says on the stray condolence cards they leave in their wake.

Detectives have long questioned why, if it was her last link with Madeleine, Mrs McCann allowed Cuddle Cat to be washed. Mrs McCann said it had simply become too grubby. It was, according to Madeleine's godfather Jon Corner, 'reeking with Madeleine's DNA'.

The sight of Kate McCann appearing for the umpteenth time, clutching a pale pink toy called Cuddles in lieu of her daughter, wrote Germaine Greer, makes me feel a bit sick.

The ghastliness of the animal–human chimera.

Fluffy pink plaything. Upkeep: minimal. Shelf-life: eternal.

He went away and made tea and when he came back the eye was eye-balling him, staring him down. He'd slipped the book onto a shelf instead of back into the pile where he found it, and now the eye on the spine – a design feature, a graphic device that had never really registered until now – was looking back out at him. It was a detail taken from the little dog on the cover. It was Fullalove's eye. But – nobody was going to believe this – it was also Madeleine's.

Madeleine's eyes that had been stylised into media emblems, notably the unusual right eye, where the pupil runs into her blue-green iris in the form of a black radial strip reaching from the pupil out to the edge of the white at the seven o'clock position, about 30 degrees clockwise from the bottom. The radial strip in the glass eye belonging to the *Fullalove* toy – in reality it was just some dark stitches fixing the eye in place in its socket – was at the eight o'clock position, at about 40 degrees. But the closeness between them was striking. Even a stranger would have said so.

It had been a controversial decision to go big on the defect in Madeleine's eye and make this her distinguishing mark, the one certain way of identifying her. Because what follows from that, if the kidnapper wants to disguise the fact that the girl with him is the girl in question? Answer:

damage the eye in some way; commit violence against the eye, maybe even remove the eye altogether, gouge it out. This was what the Policia Judiciara warned the parents could quite conceivably happen if they ignored their advice and mediafied in this way, as the father acknowledged. 'The iris is Madeleine's only true distinctive feature,' he said. 'Certainly we thought it was possible that this could potentially hurt her or' (here the interviewer noted that 'he grimaces') 'or her abductor might do something to her eye . . . But in terms of marketing it was a good ploy.'

In one of those coincidences which would never be believed if they were to happen in a novel, the man singled out by the police and – more lip-smackingly – the British media as the number-one suspect in the disappearance of Madeleine, had as his single distinguishing feature an injured eye. In folklore and popular mythology, glass eyes have had more than their share of freak appeal. And when it came to fingering Robert Murat as the Bluebeard figure in the McCann tragedy, the papers went for the noir angle with unfettered abandon.

Only Georges Bataille could write, of an eyeball removed from a corpse, that 'the caress of the eye over the skin is so utterly, so extraordinarily gentle, and the sensation is so bizarre that it has something of a rooster's horrible crowing'. But the British tabloids, writing about Murat, came close.

'A one-eyed estate agent, former car salesman and turkey-farm worker . . . Creepy oddball and obvious suspect . . . While friends and relatives portrayed suspect Robert Murat as a devoted family man, a darker picture emerged of an irritating oddball who loves to be the centre of attention . . . the one-eyed Briton . . . an underfloor chamber at Murat's home'. He was obsequious, sweated heavily, his wife had left him suddenly for reasons nobody knew, he lived with his mother, had a glass eye . . .

'With his big glass eye, vaguely uneasy manner and injudicious outbursts of self-pity' – this was one of the papers on Murat. But it was Gordon Brown's misfortune that it could just as easily have been one of the papers on the country's new partially sighted, 'psychologically flawed', Bella Lugosi-like PM.

Tony Blair's bonkers, aniseed-ball eye, as drawn by Steve Bell and other cartoonists, had always been good for a joke. Getting a laugh out of Blair, Simon Hoggart suggested on the eve of his departure, had always been 'like trying to open an oyster with a plastic fork'. So the Blair eyeball – 'the one mad staring optic' – which he seemed to have inherited from Mrs Thatcher, was a godsend: 'The bonkers eye complements the sane one, which roves around the room in a friendly way; meanwhile the angry one is taking names. Alarmingly, the eyes change places; sometimes it's the right which comes at you like a dentist's drill, sometimes the left.'

Brown's eye was not a joke. The accident which caused it was at the time catastrophic for him and it took six months lying immobile in a darkened room to save the sight of what is now considered his 'good' right eye. But being blind in one eye has proved to have serious personal and political consequences.

On television, when photographed in left profile (something his media handlers try to avoid) it can make him seem cold and unresponsive. And because his notes have to be printed in large type, it means that when he answers 'yes', for example, to a question about whether he can truly put his hand on his heart and say that bad polls had nothing to do with his decision not to call an election, he can be seen to be lying, because the words 'saw polls' on his notes are being picked up by the TV cameras and high-lighted for reproduction in the morning papers.

Seven: the number of openings to the human head – two ears, two nostrils, mouth, two eyes.

'I remember once getting really terrified that I could only see out of my eyes. I realised I am trapped in the dark inside my own body with only these two small holes to see out of,' Damien Hirst, the shark man, the cow man, the brains behind the skull, once said.

Chapter Nine

A narrative. A story. It is this, historians, political theorists and leader-writers agree, that, more than anything, a government must have if it is going to succeed. A story. A narrative to inspire supporters and enthuse the electorate.

Before a loss of the plot became the story of the Brown government as it entered only its fourth month in office, a modestly diverting storyline that had been floated was the prime minister's intention to be the head of a 'government of all the talents'.

Among the high-profile, non-Labour figures that he had recruited were TV's *Apprentice* star and business tycoon Sir Alan Sugar, who was to sit on the new Business Leaders Council, and a onetime head of the Confederation of British Industry (who, it emerged, had already discussed a possible peerage with the Tories). Brown had also signed up former deputy secretary-general of the United Nations Mark (now Lord) Mallach-Brown, and ex-naval chief Lord West as his security minister.

Getting the Swedish sporting tycoon and Tory treasurer Johan Eliasch to agree to be his 'special representative' on climate change and deforestation was regarded as a particularly bitter blow to the Conservatives, to whom Eliasch had also been a major donor. (His just-divorced wife of twenty-one years, the 'photographer, socialite and art collector' Amanda Eliasch, had just set up the love-advice website Dear Doctor Cupid, and was herself seeing 'London's Botox king' Jean-Louis Sebag. Johan Eliasch, meanwhile, was with 'the full-bodied but high-minded Ana Paula Junquiera, a plugged-in UN worker and girl-about-town from Brazil, based in London and New York'.)

There was going to be room for both high and low in the Brown 'big tent': bling as well as hair shirts, household faces as well as grandees. But not everybody the new prime minister approached agreed to join.

Among the refuseniks was Fiona Phillips, the breakfast TV presenter and possibly the most arrhythmic celebrity contestant ever to appear on Brown's favourite Saturday-evening family viewing, *Strictly Come Dancing*. It was Phillips he had faced over the untouched tumblers of Sunny Delight on the morning his GMTV appearance was overshadowed by the tantrums and tears of Heather, Lady McCartney. Fiona Phillips was reported to have been tempted by the offer of a job as a health minister and a seat in the House of Lords, but the £400,000 salary she would have to wave goodbye to meant she had to say no.

An attractive young tellyworld personality he did manage to coax on-board, however, was Tanya Byron, who had recently made a name for herself in the new niche area of

TV parenting shows, first with a programme called *Little Angels* and later with *The House of Tiny Tearaways*. Described as 'the responsible face of media parenting', she was a clinically trained psychologist with seventeen years' experience in the NHS and was appointed to lead an investigation into the impact on children of violent or sexual media imagery. Like Kate McCann, she was thirty-nine; also like Kate McCann, she worked at a GP practice, treating children with behavioural and emotional problems, which was the job Kate McCann had said, when the time was right, she wanted to retrain to do.

(Again like Mrs McCann, and her husband, Tanya Byron was having to learn how to straddle being both a clinician and a celebrity. One newspaper profiler noted 'the lavish airbrushed publicity shots', the convertible outside her house with the personalised number plate DR TAN, and marvelled at a world 'where fame and glamour sit so easily alongside ordinary life'.)

By far the most interesting thing about Byron, though, as far as much of the press was concerned, was the fact that her husband Bruce played DC Terry Perkins in *The Bill*.

And thus continued a tradition going back at least as far as Elsie Tanner and Harold Wilson in the 1960s, when Wilson was hitching his star to all things popular (populist) and northern in the heyday of the Fab Four and Beatlemania. Bill Roache, Ken Barlow in *Coronation Street* from day one, now the *Street*'s longest-lived character, used to do warm-ups for the Conservatives and Mrs Thatcher. (And Tanya Byron's soap roots even predate

Harold Wilson to the Fifties, when her father, for years head of drama at ATV, worked on *Emergency Ward 10*, forerunner of *Casualty*, and *Z Cars*, gritty black-and-white northern predecessor of *The Bill*.)

Going over the published accounts of Brown and Blair's fabled meeting at the Granita restaurant in Islington in May 1994, at which they either did or did not agree that Blair would hand over power halfway through any second Labour term, he kept returning to a footnote to one of them which mentioned that the actress Susan Tully, Michelle Fowler in *EastEnders* and one of the great British tabloid staples at that point, the Pat Phoenix of her day, had also been having dinner in Granita on the night of the Blair-Brown 'deal'.

Should he call her to try to persuade her to see him?

It was easy enough to get a number for an agent. But what did he say? How did she know he wasn't one of the rabid tribe of lurkers and watchers, the whip-and-chain collectors and morgue attendants who pursued her and pestered her with crank mail while she was a schoolgirl (still the schoolgirl she had played in *Grange Hill*), on the cusp of turning into a sexually aware young woman, one of the core 'journeys' in the early days of the show? Or part of the smaller group who routinely track her now through Flickr and Popbitch and TrashTalk, through YouTube and Google?

'Ever fancied bein' in novels? I can get you in a novel, 'Chelle.' How did *he* know he wasn't one of their kind; that anorak breed?

(Pat Phoenix recorded that, even in earlier times, meeting your public could sometimes prove to be a perilous undertaking: 'It sometimes happens in a crush when people press close to you that your arms literally disappear into the crowd as people grasp your hands. The majority are lovely, loving people but you get the occasional nutcase in the frantic crush that bends your fingers back till you think they're going to break.')

He did have a large autograph collection when he was very young, and once made Helen Shapiro cry.

'Actually, there was a guy standing in that doorway over there just before you got here,' she said, indicating a shadowy recess next door to the Red Fort Indian restaurant in Soho. 'Telephoto lens, poppin' off some shots. Thought I couldn't see what he was up to, but I could. I met Anita Dobson for lunch here the other day an' there was half a dozen of them crawlin' all over in no time. Word went round we must be goin' back in the show.'

At her suggestion, they had arranged to meet at the Soho Theatre in Dean Street. Outside the Soho Theatre, that is, at a pavement table on the other side of the window from the bar, where she could smoke. It wasn't especially warm, and it meant they were easy meat for the addicts and beggars and the large population of street-dwellers in the area. 'But,' she said, holding up a cigarette, a voice that sounded like it had never left 'Stenders', a rich wave of smoke rip-curling over the mouthpiece of the phone which she was checking for messages, 'gotta have these.' Doop-doop-beep, speed-dial call, no answer, a 'fuck it' under her breath. 'So gwawn then, what's it all about, this novel? Howds'it s'posed to work?'

She no longer acts. She has built up an alternative career as a director. (Her apprentice work included directing Dr Tan's husband, Bruce Byron, in many episodes of *The Bill*.) She went to school in Islington, close to the fleet-ingly popular Granita restaurant (now long-gone), and is a product of the Anna Scher children's theatre, which is where a lot of the lively kids from her area went and got fast-tracked into children's TV and commercials.

It was her conviction that she was only any good at playing herself - that she had really only ever played her-self, first in *Grange Hill*, and then as TV's most famous single mother, Michelle Fowler — that prompted her to throw in the towel at *EastEnders* after ten years. She was one of the soap's original characters, appearing in the first episode in February 1985 and remaining central to the series until 1995.

So now she was a director. She had stopped appearing in front of the cameras. But every so often her past — that person she used to be — will leap out and mug her. It had happened just the week before while she was watching Andrew Marr's television history of post-war Britain. One minute it was prime ministers and affairs of state, and the next minute there *she* was, with her mullet and her bad complexion, a fag on, the mouth going, giving it 'Chelle. It used to be that, even as a performer, your image receded as you grew older. But now the uniquely twenty-first-century experience is that it just replicates and multiplies in accordance with that law of the digital realm that states that anything digital will be copied, and anything copied once will fill the universe.

She filled the universe. A colleague had logged her onto to YouTube for the first time that very afternoon and the fact that just tapping the words 'Michelle Fowler' into the thing could bring so many moments of the past crowding back – a pandemonium of fragments (an aggregation of fragments is the only kind of whole we have now) – was like . . . *Pffffffffffff.* Jeeezus. You know? Can you imagine? Back from out of where was this? Sorry? Creeped her well out. F'sake.

She was sixteen when she went into *EastEnders*, and twenty-six when she left. Being sixteen, and earning silly money, she'd bring all her friends into the West End every Friday night, chatted up all the bouncers, got them all nodded into everywhere free, had a great old falling-about caper. She went on like that for three years, until she was nineteen. But then when she turned nineteen it all stopped. 'I knew the day would come when the bouncers didn't recognise me any more, and I wanted out before that happened.' End of.

Same thing seven years later, same abrupt termination, when she decided to get out of *'Stenders* after ten years. She was terrified of becoming a Ken Barlow. Or, alternatively, of hanging on until the programme-makers decided to kill her off. She made the decision and got out, much as Blair didn't, until the circumstances made it obvious he had to go. 'As a former-celebrity' is how he said he expected to be remembered, just weeks before he finally packed up and went. But this flippancy had only been arrived at after the working through of what some of those closest to him (they were rumoured to be Alastair Campbell and Philip Gould) had described as a 'psychological problem' about turning his back on Number 10.

On the night of the big Granita pow-wow in May, 1994, Sue Tully was top tabloid totty, less than a year away from chucking it all in. Brown and Blair were two men in suits wrangling over who would get the cowboy outfit and who would get the Meccano set when/if they ended seventeen years of Conservative government in three, maybe four years' time. In other words, all eyes were on her, which is why she was sitting (as she always sat in those days) with her back to the room. It took her friend Mark, who she had been at Anna Scher with, to draw her attention to the Blair–Brown bozos looking conspiratorial at a table next to the exposed-brick rear wall.

She reached across for his notebook and drew him a diagram – door here, bar in the far corner where they were, a narrow room, tables just so, another Upper Street restaurant, she'd zigzagged her way down all the halfway-decent restaurants in that road.

But then for some reason – she's never been able to quite say why – when Mark tipped her off they were leaving, she threw herself at the door. She squeezed past the people at the other tables and stood and watched the two of them walking together past the King's Head in the direction of Highbury, Tony and Gordon, at swim in the delicious uncertainties of their fate, apparently relaxed and on good terms.

The next day, or maybe the day after, there was a diary item in the *Evening Standard* getting it all arse-backwards as usual, saying that the Labour rivals Brown and Blair had taken time out from juking each for the vacancy created at the top of the party by the untimely death of John Smith ten days earlier, to have dinner with outspoken *EastEnders* star Susan Tully at the fashionable Granita restaurant on Islington's trendy Upper Street.

Were they having a laff? The confusion, she has come round to believing, stemmed from the fact that a couple of years earlier she had done a turn for Neil Kinnock on the eve of the General Election of 1992, which Kinnock had gone into as favourite but ended up losing dismally to John Major, the man who replaced Thatcher.

The event she agreed to appear at was held in Kinnock's constituency in Wales. It was a week or so after his rock-style stadium rally in Sheffield, which had been ill-judged and rubbished enough to make him lose the election just by itself. And now, just a few hours before the polls were due to open, he was welcoming the motor-mouthed, lurex-suited one, Ben Elton, and the lovely twenty-three-year-old coping lone-parent from *EastEnders* into his own back yard.

She was picked up at her home in London by an old Labour hand and practised her speech on him all the way: he encouraged her to add references to Labour being the protectors of the NHS and providers of new schools and so forth, and it seemed to go down well with a partisan audience (an audience that believed Labour was about to be swept into power in a matter of only 24 hours); it seemed to hit the spot as far as she could tell, from the reaction she got. And, even though she found out later that Kinnock himself knew that night he was going to lose and that his nine years as leader were over – he had been shown the figures and knew three days before the vote that John Major was going to win – still he elbowed through the throng to the bar where she was queuing to buy a vodka and tonic, shooed them all out of the way and brought back the vod-ton himself. Afterwards she sat next to him on the top table at dinner – her, then Neil, then Glenys, then Ben Elton – and all he had wanted to know about was herself. This little man with the knowing wink and the laddo smile and the freckled head like a linnet's egg who had suspected he was done for when they got rid of Thatcher, the woman Sue blamed for her father's redundancy from his job as a watch-case maker in Hatton Garden in 1979, the year Thatcher came to power.

Her Granita experience had an unexpected postscript.

Nine years later, in 2003, when Blair had been prime minister for seven years (and was showing no sign of keeping his part of the bargain with Brown, if there was one), she was having lunch with her agent Anna Scher in a Turkish restaurant in Upper Street. The restaurant was immediately opposite the premises where Granita used to be, and pretty soon after sitting down she could see from the blackout curtains, the lights and so on, that filming was in progress. Of course it was Stephen Frears filming *The Deal*, with Michael Sheen as Tony Blair and David Morrissey as Gordon Brown.

When they had finished eating, Anna, who has known Stephen forever, insisted on going over. 'Daaaaaaahhhh-ling!' It was one of those. But all the time he was embracing Anna, Tully could see that his eyes were locked on her.

In the finished film it is a glammed-up version of herself – 'more like Martine McCutcheon' – who sweeps into the restaurant where Cassius and Brutus are plotting. The script has TB turning to GB at that point: 'Now that – *that's* power. Twenty million viewers.'

That was one example of the coincidences, traceable through the novels of Dickens to Virginia Woolf to Anthony Powell, that can happen in a city as big as London, the sheer teeming variety of city life, Clarissa still perched on the kerb and Big Ben ringing the hour, the plangent interplay between isolation and connection. A certain excitement over the daily renewal of vital energies in a city like London.

And as they were sitting on the pavement chatting, the notebook where she had diagrammed Granita still open between them, they shared a further experience of city serendipity, of that kind of coincidence.

The *Today* programme presenter James Naughtie's book had provided the basis for Frears' film. It had also alerted him to the fact that Sue Tully from *EastEnders* had also been eating at Granita that night. And now, as they sat there with their drinks, this same Naughtie, looking pushed, maybe late in getting home to the Ellie to whom his book is dedicated, with love, maybe just a case of meetings being backed up (or being in danger of missing his cue for a concert he was due to introduce live from the Albert Hall – he also did that on Radio 3), Jim Naughtie came dashing towards them and flagged down a taxi a matter of inches from where they were sitting. She was in his book. The book was in his bag, along with fresh pasta, parmesan and other provisions from Camisa whose smells for some time had been making him feel hungry.

The closest I ever came to Tony Blair was on a train travelling from Manchester to London on a Saturday morning in late January 1993. I can be sure of the date because the story I had been in Manchester covering ran in the *Observer* two weeks later.

Blair had just been given the Home Office job by John Smith. Labour were still in opposition, but he was on the way up. ('Oh, yes, young Tony, *very*, *very* keen!' Kinnock had once been heard to joke of the barrister who he had just made a junior minister.)

A few hours before running in to Blair on the train I had been in a crack-house in what the paper called the 'ganglands' of Moss Side. I had been with 'Maz' and 'Rodney' (their real identities had to be kept hidden) and a photographer with very good contacts in Manchester, called Ged.

A few days earlier, a fourteen-year-old, Benji Stanley,

had been gunned down at a takeaway counter in Moss Side.

Like many people, Rodney claimed to know who was responsible for the murder, but nobody was talking.

Rodney described himself as 'a thief, a robber, a gangster', and also 'a tidier-upper': 'If a weapon's used, I believe in cutting it up and destroying it. Any weapon. If you walk and weapons get let off, I'll be there, making sure that all the magazines and bullets are picked up.' They weren't playing at this. These were scary characters. (Rodney would later be crippled for life in a bungled armed raid on a Securicor van picking up the takings from a supermarket.)

It had been a long night. At around 3 a.m. I had had to count £50 notes into the hands of a dealer of crack cocaine and then watch while Rodney and Maz got off their faces smoking it from a plastic Coke bottle 'works' while Ged got his pictures. Later they posed in the narrow-mesh masks and balaclavas and combat gear of 'field intelligence majors', toting Uzis and pump-action shotguns.

I was in need of a shower and was tired. I had met a writer from another paper on the train and we were talking when Blair got on. He was seen off by a group of what were probably Party workers which included a group of women who he mwah-mwhaed on both cheeks before the doors closed.

The train had barely had time to pull out of Piccadilly station before he had his head buried in a book. It was a big fat volume and he had obviously been dying to get back to it. He was about halfway through. Stockport. Crewe. Warrington Bank Quay. No other passengers came into the carriage. There was only the three of us. He never looked up.

Of course we were keen to know what he found so compelling. And, after about an hour, when he got up to go to the toilet, I took my chance.

Braced against any sudden lurches of the train, I slalomed down the aisle and grabbed a look at the cover: *Richard Milhous Nixon: The Rise of an American Politician*, by Roger Morris. I felt the ridges of the presidential seal of office punched onto the cover before I read the words. I noted the number of the page. It was a number I carried for many years in my head until it became confused with many other numbers of PINs and passwords and the various keys for living a normal online life; just some data scooped up and washed away on the information tide.

Late in the summer, as a sign that he was history, a local 'heritage' plaque went up on the wall outside the Dun Cow: 'The Prime Minister, the Rt. Hon. Anthony Lynton Blair while touring his constituency welcomed the President of the United States of America, George W. Bush, Friday 21st November, 2003 to dine in the restaurant during a visit to the United Kingdom'.

Around the same time a much larger sign like a big bib went up across the front of Minsters which aroused a great deal of local resentment. In large letters it announced that

Minsters, so long the mirror Sedgefield used to look at itself, was now under new management. It would be re-opening soon as an Indian restaurant, function room available, parties welcome.

Chapter Ten

'Is that the one with the pigeons in it?'

An Australian family had got on just before the bus left St Andrew's bus station in Edinburgh: mother, father, two boys, all open-faced, strapping, excited to be in Europe (although it would become clear, as the bus dawdled its way to the Firth of Forth and the road bridge across to where the PM's constituency home is at North Queensferry, that the mother was originally from Scotland).

The parents sat in the seat behind him, the boys, who were probably aged about nine and eleven, together in a seat across the aisle from them. Occasionally a tube of sweets would make its way, hand to hand along the row, from one side of the bus to the other. They seemed to have an easy, uncomplicated relationship. ('Ah, careful now, better sit back down, little buddy,' the father would say whenever the younger boy stood up to get a better view of something out of the window. A schoolyard full of children – boys as well as girls – wearing kilts was one thing that propelled him to his feet. And then when the rust-red spans of the railway bridge suddenly sprang up and started running parallel to the bridge they were all on across the Firth – or was it the Forth? It was a question the boy asked. None of them knew the answer.)

The wife was softly spoken; she knew how easy it was to listen in to other people's conversations on these buses. But her husband was unabashed. They had been talking about the days they had just had in London, and Piccadilly Circus, and that was when he had asked the question about the pigeons: 'Is that the one with the pigeons in it?'

It was easy to scoff, of course. And that's what he had done a few days earlier when, bizarrely, he had overheard the same conversation while sitting on the top deck of a number 22 bus travelling along Shaftesbury Avenue.

A London girl was rather dutifully pointing out things of interest to her Canadian (possibly American, but almost certainly Canadian) cousin. They were heading in the direction of Piccadilly Circus, and she mentioned this. And that is when the cousin had said (as the Australian on the bus to North Queensferry would a few days later): 'Is that the one with the pigeons?'

Tiger Tiger, the site of the so recently attempted bomb atrocity, going by on the left, went unmentioned.

But, back on the main route, the London girl pointed out Fortnum & Mason in the near-distance. 'Oh, okay,' the Canadian said, in her bored, sing-song way. 'We have one of them. It's a kind of franchise, right?'

He had felt irritated that day. Irrationally angry. It was

the kind of conversation worth carrying an iPod for, just to shut it out.

But four days later, hearing the same snippet of conversation repeated between Australians travelling through the suburbs of Edinburgh, he didn't feel angry at all. He thought it was funny. Because in the meantime he had found himself all at sea in a major city, not knowing his Princes Street from his Royal mile, his Old Town from his New Town.

Only the night before, trying to find his way from his hen-coop of a room that he had booked a the last minute on the internet, to Waverley Station (a distance of less than a mile, roughly the distance from the eastern end of Shaftesbury Avenue to Fortnum's) he had twice had to stop pedestrians and ask them to show him where he was on the map.

'This part of it – the waiting and watching, looking for "something to happen", like staring at the empty page, waiting for "inspiration", some characters, a story – is part of the project.' He had written this in his notebook over dinner – a dreary dinner in a terrible pizza place. But it wasn't. It was just being adrift in a strange place without having any real idea of what it was you were doing there. He didn't even know at that point that there was a railway station at North Queensferry – that there was a quick mainline connection from Edinburgh and that it was a well-used commuter stop: Gordon Brown's stop for many years – and so had ended up taking the bus.

Madeleine's face was up on the TV monitors in the bus station. Her father was Scottish. Her auntie Phil and her uncle John, her father's sister and brother, both familiar now in the media for their part in the campaign to find Madeleine, Philomena in particular for the warm rapport she was supposed to have established with the prime minister, a Fife man, were Scottish. The website was being run from a tiny town up on the east coast by one of auntie Phil's former pupils. Gerry had been over the week before to appear at the Edinburgh Television Festival, interviewed by Kirsty Wark.

But the housewives and little old ladies who might once have gathered in small groups and speculated on the fate of 'the poor wee mite' now hardly looked up, or if they did seemed impatient for the picture of Madeleine to flip over and for the more vital information about departure times and boarding bays to come back up.

They were witness to the more general shift from initial shock and intensity of feeling, to an alienated separatedness that was becoming apparent, a distancing.

Heading along Princes Street, the bus passed the National Galleries of Scotland whose venerable, mossy columns had been clad in once garish, now weatherbeaten Campbell's soup cans about two metres tall. The effect was slightly ludicrous, like one of Muriel Spark's Kelvinside ladies arriving for tea at the tea-rooms wearing Spandex trousers and pop-sox.

The soup cans were there to advertise a travelling Andy Warhol retrospective, which he had been to see the day before. He had been powerfully reminded by the images in the 'Death and Disaster' series, and by the famous repeated images of Jacqueline Onassis and Elizabeth Taylor and the many melancholic, corrupted Marilyns, of Kate McCann, snapped over and over in the flat bright light of Praia da Luz. Two big themes, in many ways the themes that have defined the world since 'Camelot' and Kennedy and that Warhol was smart enough to cotton on to before anybody: Glamour and Death.

'The death series I did was divided into two parts,' Warhol once said, 'the first one famous deaths and the second one people nobody ever heard of, and I thought that people should think about them sometimes. It's not that I feel sorry for them, it's just that people go by and it doesn't really matter to them that someone unknown was killed. I still care about people but it would be so much easier not to care. It's too hard to care. I want to care but it's so hard.'

The brutal fact of violent death. Kate McCann's slim, blonde, disciplined Jackie-O standard of beauty; her dawn runs on the beach; her friendliness to the camera. The levelling sameness with which real, not symbolic, death erupts into daily life.

Faced with these paintings – car crashes, suicides, state execution, death-stalked celebrity – one might take seriously, if only for a moment, Warhol's dictum that in the future everyone will be famous for fifteen minutes, wrote Thomas Crow, but conclude that in his eyes it was likely to be under fairly horrifying circumstances.

The curiously intimate knowledge the world garners about an unknown figure.

MM. Madeleine McCann. Marilyn Monroe.

Everything I know about a woman who is dead and whom I didn't know.

'How are you feeling? Excited?' the Australian in the seat behind asked his wife.

'I don't know,' she said. 'Strange.'

'I'm feeling excited,' he said.

'Why?'

'About seeing Dunfermline. About seeing that part of your past. Putting in another little part of the puzzle about you.'

The rust-red Forth railway bridge, triple-dinosaur construction, like three dinosaurs with necks and tails entwined, rose up on the right. They all – husband and wife, both sons – had digital cameras, and they took pictures of the bridge, and then pictures of each other taking pictures of the bridge spanning the water which they were just then suspended over themselves.

'Are you going to look up your dad?' he said when it had all settled down.

'No,' she said. There was a silence. 'No.'

Once on the other side of the water from Edinburgh, the sign saying 'North Queensferry' pointed left, but the bus turned right and pulled in after about a mile at Inver-keithing services. There was no scheduled stop at North Queensferry, it seemed, for this particular bus, but he was told by a friendly man in the ticket office that it was easily walkable from there, and so he set off.

It was a warm day, and it was a steep hill that, at this Inverkeithing end of things, was unexpectedly rough-and-ready, with a bathroom-fittings cash-and-carry and an oily-rag garage with loud music thudding out of it. Further on, perspiring now, the sun directly overhead, he passed an abandoned quarry.

It was only near the brow of the hill, where the view opened out across the water back towards Edinburgh and east towards the small humped islands of Bass Rock and Berwick Law, that the houses started to look like they belonged to 'the very best' part of North Queensferry, which he had read was what this was.

Going up the hill, he couldn't shake off the feeling that he was encroaching. Not on Gordon Brown, the prime minister, because this was a public road, and he had every right to be on it (although he would discover very quickly that the local police, still jittery under the burden of their newly imposed responsibility and having to get used to special fire-arms officers brought in from other constabularies, would aggressively dispute this).

He also knew that Brown was not at home. This was a Thursday. The previous day the prime minister had taken his place in Parliament Square for the unveiling of a statue to Nelson Mandela. On Friday he would be in the Guards

Chapel in central London for the service to mark the tenth anniversary of the death of Princess Diana. He was then going to join the Queen and her family for the weekend at Balmoral.

No, the encroachment he felt, padding up Ferryhill Road, was on another writer – somebody he knew; a writer who in the past he had a sometimes shaky relationship with, and who, in a long autobiographical essay and numerous pieces of journalism, had described his home village into existence, meat pie by meat pie, whin bush by whin bush, rivet by rivet. Approaching it, he felt as any writer might feel trespassing the boundary into Roth's Newark, New Jersey, say, or Naipaul's Trinidad or the tiny piece of Wiltshire near Stonehenge that Naipaul evokes with such clarity and directness in *The Enigma of Arrival*.

His first engagement with the police came when he was sizing up a large house behind a high stone wall and just deciding that the basket-ball hoop with backboard in the drive ruled it out as anywhere Brown might live. The two officers were young and wearing protection vests with automatic rifles slung across them. They asked if they could help and he said, yes, they could point him in the direction of the prime minister's house. They asked for ID and he told them he didn't have any (which, other than credit cards, he didn't). Asked to explain the purpose of his visit, he told them that this was proving to be a summer of disappearances, absences, some voluntary, others not; that he was interested in the idea of absence, of erasure and self-erasure. He said he found it more interesting to look at the prime minister's house without him in it, in a way, than if he was actually there. Erasure, like rubbing out? But instead of looking alarmed, they looked sceptical at this, and allowed him to continue on his way.

Dramcarling, the house that Gordon Brown bought in North Queensferry in 1990, is one of a string of Victorian villas near the station which had been built speculatively in an attempt to woo commuters across the new bridge from Edinburgh. Unusually for a villa built in late Victorian Scotland, as this other writer who grew up in North Queensferry has of course already pointed out (he used to deliver papers to the Brown house as a boy), the walls are unrendered red brick and the roof flat. 'You might even say it was a cautious kind of house.'

Dramcarling, in the event, identified itself. To the right, as he looked at it, were the first signs of the police beginning to dig in – some wire-mesh screens, some temporary, lightweight crowd-control barriers – like a junior, starter version of the bomb-detection portals and robotic inspection systems, the defensive architecture then in the process of being stripped away from the Blairs' place in Sedgefield.

The significant difference was that Myrobella is situated in a copse, in a natural valley, folded away.

Dramcarling is raised aloft. Brown had bought it for the view it gives across the Firth of Forth towards Arthur's Seat and the castle. But now he was finding more and more that *he* was the view. It wasn't a glimpse of the bridges mirrored in the water the folks in the idling cars were wanting to catch, but one of the PM in an intimate, unguarded moment, maybe hoofing a ball about with John and Fraser. Many people now will turn their backs on the view to gaze instead at the double-fronted villa in its enviable position on the crest of the hill and remember that Brown's wedding to Sarah Macaulay, kept secret from everybody until the last minute, performed by the Church of Scotland minister from the local kirk in Inverkeithing, took place in the living room in front of a very few close friends and family, the bride elegantly attired in an ivory two-piece silk suit, the bridegroom in his usual rumpled suit with regulation red tie, the scrambled photo-call in the back garden that included an exchanged kiss between Mr and Mrs Brown 'of some awkwardness', leaving for his American honeymoon in his brother's car.

There are few more authentic pictures of the real Brown than those from his wedding, wrote Naughtie, portraits of a man uncomfortable at the mingling of the public and private, ill at ease with the expected opening-up of a life for public observation and comment.

And now, all around Dramcarling, the barriers were really going up. Brown was being further closed off.

It was as if the high-visibility representatives of his heightened security were policing the perimeter of the prime minister's psyche rather than merely the boundary of the 'dream home' with the dream view – his old books from his student days still lined up on the living-room mantelpiece as if he was still in a student let; the armchairs comfortably shabby – to which he still retreats at every possible opportunity.

The grid of fifty million and the grid of intimacy.

There is a national life, and intimate life. The distance between these two grids is very great. There is one method, one brutal and shocking method – Oswald used it, Sirhan-Sirhan, the Chapman who killed John Lennon – of connecting the two.

Today, in late August, he remained vulnerable to sinister Fiats and Toyota Corollas, the roadblocks, the pre-bomb cordons, the panoptical surveillance not yet in place.

These musings were interrupted by a burly polis who had materialised at the left-hand side of the house and was beckoning to him from the slope of the prime minister's front garden, indicating for him to step across the road and meet him at the gate.

'D'you mind me asking what your business is here today, sir?'

'I'm a writer.'

'Oh aye, a writer? What kind of writing?'

'Fiction. Non-fiction. Some journalism.'

'S'at right? The papers. You won't mind my asking where you stopped last night?'

'In a hotel. In Edinburgh. Not very pleasant. I can't remember the name.'

'Oh, you cannae? Can you show me some ID?'

This was the third time in under an hour he had been asked to prove his identity. The first two officers who had asked him about his business and seemed satisfied with his answers had in fact soon followed him in a police Range Rover and pulled him over to the side of the road so that further particulars – address, phone number, date of birth – could be taken.

Now the burly polisman was wanting to take his picture. He had produced a little hand-held device (he knew it was called a Web'n'Walk, his wife had the same model) from out of one of his many pockets – he was a walking trade fair of rifles, pistols, handcuffs, body armour and so on – and was tapping at it with the stylus provided which looked incongruously dainty, like a splinter in his big hands.

He positioned him in front of the unpruned box hedge at Dramcarling but then experienced a non-connection or a malfunction because nothing happened, the screen remained blank. He made some suggestions and the polis got his picture.

'Ach,' he said. 'Too much sky.'

'D'you want to have another go? Shall I take my sunglasses off?'

'Cheers.'

'Can I have a look? . . . Oh, best picture I've had taken in a long time.'

He had a relation working as a body-protection officer with the police in the north-east that one of the clean-cut pair of younger constables had reminded him of. He had received a group email from Michael a few days earlier –

joky, he imagined, and in dubious taste, as they usually were – called 'The International Rules of Manhood', which he had saved unopened.

But he had a while to wait for the train – he had located the station on the other side of the hill from Brown's house and had decided to return by train to Edinburgh instead of the slow trip back on the bus – so he opened 'The International Rules of Manhood' and began scrolling through it.

THE INTERNATIONAL RULES OF MANHOOD

1: Under no circumstances may two men share an umbrella.

2: It is OK for a man to cry ONLY under the following circumstances:
   (a) When a heroic dog dies to save its master
   (b) The moment Angelina Jolie starts unbuttoning her blouse
   (c) After wrecking your boss's car
   (d) One hour, 12 minutes, 37 seconds into *The Crying Game*
   (e) When she is using her teeth . . .

7: No man shall ever be required to buy a birthday present for another man. In fact, even remembering your buddy's birthday is strictly optional. At that point, you must celebrate at a strip bar of the birthday boy's choice . . .

9: When stumbling upon other guys watching a sporting event, you may ask the score of the game in progress, but you may never ask who's playing.

10: You may flatulate in front of a woman only after you have brought her to climax. If you trap her head under the covers for the purpose of flatulent entertainment, she's officially your girl-friend . . .
14: Friends don't let friends wear Speedos. Ever. Issue closed . . .
17: A man in the company of a hot, suggestively dressed woman must remain sober enough to fight.

In his cover note Michael had written, 'Pay particular attention to rules 23, 24 and 27':

23: Never allow a telephone conversation with a woman to go on longer than you are able to have sex with her. Keep a stopwatch by the phone. Hang up if necessary.
24: The morning after you and a girl who was formerly 'just a friend' have carnal, drunken monkey sex, the fact that you're feeling weird and guilty is no reason for you not to nail each other again before the discussion about what a big mistake it was occurs.
27: The girl who replies to the question 'What do you want for Christmas?' with 'If you loved me, you'd know what I want!' gets an Xbox. End of story.
The International Council of Manhood Ltd

*

Early in the morning following his trip to North Queensferry, his wife was woken by a man who said he was from the power company. When she opened the door she was confronted by two T-shirted men who looked like bouncers or SAS and who, after stepping briefly into the flat, and failing to produce any identification, hurriedly made their excuses and left.

She was concerned enough to phone EDF Energy who said they had no knowledge of anybody being sent. A further call to an emergency number also drew a blank.

On the morning of his first full day in office, Gordon Brown rose to the news that three more British soldiers had been killed in Iraq, with several more seriously injured. Among the dead were two twenty-year-olds: privates Jamie Kerr from Cowdenbeath, and Scott Kennedy, known to all as 'Casper', from Dunfermline. They were serving with the Black Watch, they were 'Fifers' like himself, they and their families were his constituents.

They died with a third soldier when a roadside bomb exploded near Basra.

They were returning from a re-supply mission to Basra Palace around 1 a.m. and had stepped from their Warrior armoured vehicle when insurgent members of a 'rogue militia' set off an improvised explosive device.

Jamie Kerr's page on Bebo was inundated with tributes from devastated friends who had just heard of his death. One said, 'RIP Jamie Kerr. I can't believe you're gone, hunnie. Sleep tight. Night night.'

Another said, 'Love you mate. You were a great guy. Never forget your happy face'.

Jamie regularly updated his page on the Bebo website, keeping in touch with the people he had left back home. Shortly before he died, he wrote: 'You may ask why I am writing this [at 5 a.m. in Basra]. Well . . . canny get any . . . sleep and a want to go hame!'

John Stonham (screen name 'stonebollocks'), serving with the Argyll and Sutherland Highlanders overseas, was lucky enough to get home, but only just. Blown up in a car-bomb attack in the Iraqi town of Shibah in 2004, he was in a coma for nineteen days and given little chance of surviving the flight from Iraq to Britain.

But, twenty-seven operations later, in 2007 he was still living and 'back up on ma feet an walking wae a crutch', he emailed his chatroom friends.

Stonebollocks's Bebo profile in part reads:

Sports: none am a cripple, according to the sun.
Scared Of: iraqi petrol tanker drivers, size 18 catheter's.
Happiest When: on ma morphine patches, when the m.o.d admitted liabilty, its set me up for life.
Hate: . . . the blue dress thats does up at the back, u need to wear b4 an op (how vulnerable do u feel in that).
Hometown: erskine hospital

'Its all good,' John Stonham writes, 'take it fae me lifes to short to dwell on things. Share the luv.'

*

Erskine is on the outskirts of Glasgow. It is where John Smeaton lives with Mum, Catherine, and Dad, Iain, and from where he makes the easy commute to Glasgow airport to work. It is to 'stonebollocks' and the other residents of Erskine Hospital, formerly the Princess Louise Hospital for Limbless Soldiers and Sailors – there are in fact a number of 'Erskines' in various locations in Scotland, dedicated to the care of older servicemen and servicewomen, as well as the casualties of the new wars of Iraq and Afghanistan – it was to 'the real heroes' back from Iraq that Smeato passed on the thousands of pints put behind the counter for him by people using their credit cards and PayPal.

Erskine Hospital was opened in 1916 to help treat the tens of thousands of British veterans who were disabled during the carnage of the First World War. A desperate shortage of artificial limbs was the great pressing problem of those years. It was ingeniously resolved by harnessing the skills of the workers of the nearby Clyde shipyards and soon the Erskine limb had been devised.

No one then could have envisaged that there would still be a need for 'Erskine care' nearly a century later or that it would be required to extend it to the treatment of soldiers traumatised by being targets of suicide bombers graduated from Quran study groups in gritty neighbourhoods of Brooklyn and south London, or *madrasas* in Wakefield; or from having to scrape the brains of a best friend off their combat jacket or watching children shot dead as human shields or living for six months in constant fear of their lives.

By July 2006, according to the *New York Times*, there were an estimated 6,000 checkpoints in Baghdad, manned by 51,000 soldiers and police, yet car bombers were still setting off deadly explosions on an almost daily basis; the city was rocked by several kamikaze or remote-detonated bombs virtually every day. By June 2005, it was estimated that some 500 car bombs had killed or wounded more than 9,000 people in Iraq, with 143 car-bomb attacks in May 2005 alone.

The modern car bomb: the use of an inconspicuous vehicle, anonymous in almost any urban setting, to transport large quantities of high explosive into precise range of a high-value target. Known as 'the poor man's air force'. A creative atrocity, and something those airlifted home from Basra and Shibah and Helmand Province and other points of planet Jihad had good reason to think they had left far behind.

And then in summer 2007 it followed them home. All that remained of the suicide bomber was a charred forearm handcuffed to a steering wheel. Burning fuel instantly engulfed the market and nearby homes. A white Mitsubishi sedan exploded in a huge fireball. The fire chased the people down and ate them alive.

Some of the suicide attacks were beyond horrific. The car bomb that rammed the gate and exploded at the steps of the lobby, the flocks of hungry crows hovering over a rubble composed of car parts, shredded clothing, and dismembered bodies. Suicide bombers cruising the streets in search of targets of opportunity. A sports utility vehicle registered in Texas. A foot taped to the accelerator. The eagerness of foreign volunteers, especially large numbers of Saudis and Jordanians, to martyr themselves in flame and molten metal, seeking to use car bombs as stairways to paradise.

The national threat level had been raised to 'critical', the highest degree possible, which confirmed another attack was expected imminently.

Al-Qaidist 'replicants', al-Qaida affiliates or clones, the whole horror show outside their own front door. Forty or fifty people can be massacred with a stolen car and £150-worth of bootlegged electronics.

And the people arrested were doctors. Mind-blowing, man. A total freakin mind-fuck, that one. A junior doctor, Bilal Abdulla, had worked at the Royal Alexandra Hospital in Paisley, near Glasgow, after graduating from Baghdad University three years ago.

His alleged accomplice still lay in the hospital, seriously injured and receiving treatment from the staff who had previously worked alongside the young Iraqi being questioned by police in connection with the attacks. Terror plot hatched in British hospitals. Aam *in* a British hawsptl, ken wha am sayin. It's knocked me back, like. Right enough, so it has. Its fukd ma heed.

The kind of people treating them turned out to be terrorists. Double fkn whammy, or what? Protégés at who-knew-how-many removes of Mullah Omar, the one-eyed mystic who founded the Taliban in 1992 and essentially ruled Afghanistan from 1996 until the invasion by allied forces in 2001. 'Taliban', meaning 'to teach'.

Eight of the nine people arrested for the attempted car-bomb attacks on Glasgow and London were doctors or National Health Service workers.

Ayman al-Zawahiri, the ideological leader of al-Qaida, was a doctor, one of a family of thirty-one doctors, chemists or pharmacists, and Osama bin Laden's personal physician, dug into a trench between two mountain positions.

Six of the 'Tapas 7' were doctors or had connections with the NHS. That made eight of the 'Tapas 9', when you counted Kate and Gerry McCann.

Gerry was the youngest of five children of Irish immigrants. He went on to study medicine at the University of Glasgow. Kate studied medicine at the University of Dundee. They met when they were both junior doctors at Western Infirmary in Glasgow. When she left to work in New Zealand for a year, he followed and won her heart.

Erskine Hospital. The Royal Alexandra, Paisley. Western Infirmary.

All hospitals hold a secret. According to the plan displayed in the entrance hall, the windowless ground floor of the main building contains the emergency department, operating theatres, and intensive care wards. This leaves about a third of the floor area unaccounted for, a blank on the chart where you will in fact find the morgue and the post-mortem room, a sluice room, a furnace room, a number of side rooms filled with clamps, scalpels, kidney-shaped bowls, hydraulic corpse technology: a terra incognita marked 'Histopathology'; the place where the bodies come.

The kinds of change worked by severe trauma in the minds of those who suffer its effects are beyond the ability of psychoanalysis or psychiatry or any other form of psychotherapy to repair. The number of troops who have committed suicide after serving in Iraq or Afghanistan is equivalent to 10 per cent of deaths suffered in operations. The Ministry of Defence has disclosed that seventeen serving personnel have to date killed themselves after witnessing the horrors of conflict.

The images that arrive in their mind without invitation are so clear that they seem almost as if they were happening again. They are pursued by their memories; their memories harass them, and they cannot get rid of them. A part of them came to a standstill and they are drawn back to the people they were with a frequency that is punishing.

He had been thinking about trauma, reading some things about trauma. Their experience of trauma was what the McCanns, Gordon Brown, and Brown's new friend John Smeaton, the Queen's Gallantry Medal added to his long list of trophies and citations, had in common.

Life-changing moments. Calamitous events.

For Kate McCann it was the moment of walking in and finding the bed empty, Madeleine missing, Cuddle Cat, which she had left her holding, high on a shelf where Madeleine could never have reached.

Gordon Brown lost the sight in his left eye and was almost blinded by a clash of heads in a game of rugby, that trauma leading to the trauma of his eye operations, the months in the blacked-out room listening to books for the blind, the possibility of perhaps never being able to see again.

John Smeaton saw two men in a burning car intent on killing and maiming dozens, maybe hundreds, of men, women and children; a man with his skin on fire screaming something about Allah, throwing punches at a policeman, Smeato's pal coming up to him afterwards and going, 'What did you do that for, you maddie?'

Candid news photographs are structured to reveal how people react when the comfortable facade of daily life is torn away. Facing experiences of great joy or tragic loss, people expose themselves, and photographs of such moments are thought to reveal truths of human nature.

The news. Always something – usually unpleasant – happening far away to a stranger; to somebody else, somewhere that we're lucky not to be.

The best of life is lived quietly, wrote John McGahern, where nothing happens but our calm journey through the day, where change is imperceptible and the precious life is everything.

They did not give Portuguese police the satisfaction of crying.

Chapter Eleven

Dan Weir was an apprentice paparazzo. £500 can set you up in business in these days of digitisation, and that's what he'd done. On the night the butane-and-nail-filled Mercedes saloon failed to detonate on the pavement outside Tiger Tiger in the Haymarket, Weir had been night papping. He was on his way home from patrolling the nightclub circuit when he got the snap – the green car abandoned on the pavement, boot open, gas canisters scattered around the rear wheels – that appeared in most of the following day's papers and on all the rolling-news channels. 'It's a dream shot,' he said of the picture, which was expected to make him upwards of £25,000.

On that same night, at roughly the time the emergency services were being called to Tiger Tiger and the West End was being cleared, in a Mayfair gallery little more than a hundred yards away, a standing man was spraying Windolene onto his penis and masturbating into a carrier bag.

By 28 June, Damien Hirst's piece *For the Love of God* –

the platinum impression of a skull set with thousands of small diamonds for which the artist was famously asking £50 million – had been on display at the White Cube gallery in Mason's Yard for just under a month and the show still had ten days to run.

The skull was shown in a bullet-proof, cube-shaped vitrine mounted on a metal plinth in a totally black environment – black ceiling and walls; black floor – in conditions of intense security. It was reported to be the most expensive object assembled in Britain since the Crown Jewels, and security was to Tower of London standards, and beyond.

The skull was attended by armed guards at all times.

At night it retracted into the plinth, which was also a safe, bolted to the floor. The floor had been reinforced.

There was a secret camera in the room that the men patrolling it weren't aware was there. They also didn't know that the skull was, in fact, in the room overnight with them: due to an elaborate security procedure, arrived at in collaboration with the insurers, they thought they were standing watch over an absence; that they were guarding nothing.

An armour-plated truck would arrive every evening and remove a box containing the skull for safekeeping to a vault. Every morning, the same procedure in reverse.

In fact the box was always empty. The skull never left the building.

In the small upper gallery where it was shown, an unsuspected presence – a man in black, lurking in the shadows – would step forward occasionally and request that a visitor turn off their mobile phone or, Windolene in hand, rub a cloth over the glass where the grease-marks of people's noses had started to show up. The Windolene was a typical example of Hirst's attention to detail, as well as a clue to the often-overlooked performative aspect of his work.

Two night-guards were caught sleeping by the secret camera and sacked. A third was caught masturbating into a carrier bag as the West End was being evacuated under threat of terrorist attack, within the force field of the skull, cold glass and a black pedestal, put to rest for the night in its velvet-lined, coffinated home, a glittering effigy of death, a deathly treasure moulded from the head of the insignificant man.

'The insignificant man'. This is Mark Evans's phrase.

He is managing director of Bentley & Skinner, Bond Street jewellers by appointment to the Queen and HRH the Prince of Wales. He uses it – 'the skull of the insignificant man' – to distinguish it from both the precious object to which it lends its volume – the diamond skull – and a third skull which also had a part to play in the diamond skull's journey to completion.

On the night before Hirst's both sublime and monetised invention was going to be unveiled to the world – among many things, it was the apotheosis of the recent inundation of liquidity into the art market, and art's transformation from luxury to fungible asset – Mark Evans hosted a small drinks party in his drawing-room-sized, Dickensian ('Buying and selling the loveliest jewellery for over 180 years', it was there in Dickens' day), just-this-side-of-lugubrious office over the shop.

As a rule, Mr Mark never waits upon a customer unless they ask for him. Then it is a pleasure to do so and often a privilege when a personage, for example, consults him about the resetting of family jewels or – finding themselves, ahem, in Short Street – engages him to sell them 'discreetly'.

It had been Mr Mark's pleasure to welcome the successful artist Damien Hirst into his private office on a number of occasions in the past. Though certainly different, they were comfortable with each other. '"I feel comfortable with *you guys*", I seem to remember is how he put it,' Mr Mark says of the day he asked Hirst why, of all the jewellers in London, he had chosen to ask Bentley & Skinner to carry out the commission of realising the skull, a task which involved the patient harvesting of 'conflict free' diamonds from all corners of the world.

Visitors to Mr Mark's private room are admitted via a velvet rope at the foot of a narrow winding staircase and it was a convivial atmosphere that greeted the artist and other invited guests on that evening in early June. The drinks were served in lead-crystal glasses on silver trays, and there were nibbles and inconsequential cocktail chatter, and the press of bodies for a long time obscured the little arrangement Mr Mark had organised on a fine, bow-fronted mahogany desk of the three skulls.

On a small plinth draped in burgundy velvet in the centre was the diamond skull; to its left stood the skull of the insignificant man; and on the right was a third skull sculpted from gleaming, transparent rock-crystal, a replicant of or companion-piece to the notorious Aztec rock-crystal skull that attracts a devoted audience of mumblers and rune-readers and interplanetary travellers warbling zombie-speak to the moonbeams to its room in the British Museum. Mark Evans had acquired his own version of this object of philosophical contemplation – the former 'property of a gentleman' – a matter of days before Damien Hirst came to him with his momentous commission. A premonition perhaps! An omen! What stranger than another skull!

A number of people present on the drinks evening only became aware of the tableau of the three skulls when the dowsers – two ladies in old-fashioned evening gowns, relics of a war-time concert party, and a gentleman – started dowsing, a process that consisted of much rolling of the eyes and low chanting, whites of the eyes showing, eyes rolled back up into the head, and then the metal dowsing rods going to work receiving the energy of the skulls, the enormous, almost overwhelming energies they said they felt emanating from the rock-crystal specimen, harnessing that energy and rechannelling it, the dowser rods reacting really violently, an enormous field of energy, almost jerking themselves out of their hands, redistributing the energy from the crystal skull into the dead skull of the insignificant man, whose soul had found release, they believed, a soul which until then had been agonised in some way but had finally found a passage with the advent of the diamond creation.

The diamond skull set with the teeth they had extracted from the skull of the insignificant man, a young adult male complete with dentition and mandible.

Hypoplastic defects were noted on the enamel of canines and first molars, with no other teeth displaying this change, suggesting the individual was exposed to stress between the ages of three and five years, based on banding at the root of the molars.

The skull was of excellent preservation with an even ivory colour. There were no root traces or soil residue associated with the skull, suggesting that it had either been cleaned after exhumation or had never been interred.

There were two doors that opened inwards on the bed of the pedestal underneath the skull. Every night the skull descended and the doors closed above it. All night the halogen spots continued to illuminate the space where the skull rested during daylight hours, the shape made by its base, residues of diamond dust on the dark lining like human trace.

It's there, then turn around and it's gone.

What does a mother look like when her child has been wrenched from her?

Chapter Twelve

When the twins grew up and were old enough to leave home they both went far away.

They were saturated with the news. The news ate into their faces, bit into their every pore, came into the house on the clothes of their mother and father, hung in the static around the television and the telephone, clustered round the dust motes, rising, falling, clung to the grease on the dishes in the sink. Newsnewsnews.

More news.

The girl had a restless existence. She never settled down. Zimbabwe. California. Chamonix (the ski instructor). A small moment of clarity and triumph in a dirt pit in Australia with filthy water soaking into her clothing, rats and other rodents running over her face. She had to place a bull's eyeball between her teeth and bite into it and swallow and she did it, she didn't blanch.

Attagirl! she could hear her father say. Her father was dead. And the greatest triumph: 'I don't have a number for her' – her reply when asked how her mother, the former great leader, now vulnerable and frail, was taking the ritual humiliations being meted out to her daughter nightly on prime-time TV.

The boy was always an accident waiting to happen. The boy was never much good. Poor Mark. (PODWAS – a text that went around cock-a-hoop Labour MPs in the first weeks of the Brown government, the weeks of the Brown Bounce: 'Poor Old Dave What A Shame').

KGOY. A problem for the toy industry worldwide. Kids Getting Older Younger. Blame the parents.

'They never talked about [their father and mother] . . . There was no need to,' wrote E. L. Doctorow in *The Book of Daniel*. 'They had shared an experience so evenly that to have spoken about it would have diminished what they knew and understood. Share and share alike, the cardinal point of justice for children driven home to them with vicious exactitude . . . So at the beginning at least, there was no need to talk about it. When the brother and the sister went somewhere, or did something together; when he tightened her skate or helped her with her homework, or took her to the movies; the way they moved, physically moved, in a convalescence of suffering, spoke about it. The way he would hold her arm as they ran across the street in front of traffic spoke about it. The way his muscles tensed when she wasn't where she was supposed to be at any given time of the day, that spoke of it as well.'

What then of Sean? What of Amelie?

When the twins were carried into the silver Renault Scenic rental car outside Vista do Mar on the morning that they flew home to England from Praia da Luz, they were seen to be fleshlike, pink and normal.

On emerging at the other end, however, Sean in the arms of his mother, Amelie in the arms of her father, their features had been electronically scrambled, turned into a moving mosaic. They were each wearing a mask like a tiny cathedral window fixed to their face.

What did the world look like seen through the lens of such a thing? What did they see looking back at a world gazing so hungrily and yet casually at them? A kaleidoscope. Luridly tinted, for sure. Distorted, always shapeshifting. A phantasmagoria.

'Celebrity victims'. A horrible expression. So let's not use it.

Let's leave them in the nursery in the safekeeping of Patty the Panda and Mortimer the Moose and Cuddle Cat.

Polly Pocket and Pupsqueak.

Say night-night, Sean. Say night-night, Amelie. Say night-night to Madeleine and pray God to bring her home.

Bye-bye, everybody. Bye-bye.

Acknowledgements

Like all novels, this one derives from a broad range of materials and sources. Books that proved particularly useful were: *Blair*, by Anthony Seldon; *The Rivals: The Intimate Story of a Political Marriage*, by James Naughtie; *Common Fame*, by Richard Schickel; *Buda's Wagon: A Brief History of the Car Bomb*, by Mike Davis; and, in a more oblique way, *Imagined Cities: Urban Experience and the Language of the Novel*, by Robert Alter.

'Literature is news that stays news,' Ezra Pound once said. In order for yesterday's news to become a novel while the events and characters it depicted were still fresh in people's memories, it had to be written and produced to a punishingly tight schedule. It couldn't have happened without the encouragement and total commitment of everybody at Faber from the outset. I particularly want to thank Stephen Page, Lee Brackstone, Angus Cargill, Hannah Griffiths, Dave Watkins, Donna Payne, Kate Burton, John Grindrod, Patrick Keogh and Anna Pallai. I would also like to thank everybody at the British School at Rome, where I completed the book.

G.B., February 2008